Chapter One

Sweet.

Chocolate drizzle with a hint of orange zest.

Salty.

Toasted hazelnuts with a smoky crunch.

Soft.

Dollop of pudding with vanilla bean and bourbon.

Sentiment.

Indigo violas sprinkled over the plate like a wash of spring.

Sophia Brown placed the dessert dishes in front of her guests, turning them so the pudding was at ten o'clock, the nuts in the center, the drizzle at five o'clock. She refilled glasses with champagne and sparkling cider. She returned to the kitchen to turn on the espresso machine. She listened to the clatter of silver, the murmur of voices, the hushed whispers of concern.

"Em, are you sure your mom is doing okay? She looks thin to me. She might be cooking a lot, but I don't think she's eating a lot."

"She's…quiet. Subdued. I would say that's normal under the circumstances."

Sophia smiled at the censure in her daughter's voice. The cub defends the mama lion.

"I think she'll do better now that spring is here. She's already gardening, already back to the plant nurseries. That will cheer her up." Cady's sweet voice was brimming with hope. Cub Number Two, optimistic as always.

"Well," Mrs. Anderson replied, "that may be true. But it's been a long, hard winter. And Sophia went through quite a dark period."

"She's grieving, Mrs. Anderson. People grieve after losing a spouse." Em's voice was low.

"Mom is doing all the right things. She's seeing a therapist. She's going to church. She's staying busy," Cady said.

"I'm sure you're right," Margaret Anderson answered. There was a hint of disbelief in her tone. "However, I think she needs to get out of this house. It's full of memories that must be painful—"

"Does anyone want coffee?" Sophia brought in the silver platter and placed it on the table. It was topped with cream and cubes of sugar and tiny spoons tied with satin ribbons.

Her life was unraveling. Had unraveled. Was messy, and confusing, and in complete disarray.

But hell if her table didn't look picture perfect.

At least one part of her life was still in order.

✿ ✿ ✿

"So, you see, Mrs. Brown, if we don't treat the grub problem now, you're going to have a much bigger problem in a couple of months."

Sophia leaned against the picket fence and surveyed the *leading expert in lawn care.*

"Uh-huh." She kicked her boot against a post and a large

clump of dirt flew off. "What's the much bigger problem going to be?"

The kid, probably no older than twenty-one years, shook his head sadly, as though the weight of the world had lowered itself onto his scrawny shoulders.

"Your lawn will be completely decimated."

"Hmm. Completely decimated." She wished those words had no meaning for her. Other than grubs. Other than her lawn.

"So you want to kill the grubs?"

"Of course. Of course we want to kill the grubs. Not only will they eat the roots of your turf grass, but they attract undesirable animals, such as skunks, which will rip up your whole lawn trying to eat the grubs."

If Sophia were inclined to smile, or even laugh, this young man would have elicited a chuckle. His pants were falling down, with boxer shorts proudly displayed over the waistband. He had several thick gold chains around his neck. Pimples on his cheeks. Oversized sunglasses perched on top of his head.

"Mrs. Brown? You do realize the severity of this problem. Right?"

"The grubs must be hungry. Don't you think? After this long Vermont winter? No wonder they're munching on the grass roots."

The lawn boy looked perplexed.

"And the skunks are probably hungry, too. My front yard is like a grub smorgasbord for them. They must love it."

"Do you want me to kill the skunks, too? 'Cause I can do that."

"It's a suburban cycle of life. I plant turf grass, the grubs eat the turf grass, the skunks eat the grubs, and I'm left with a pile of dirt in my front yard."

"Mrs. Brown…are you okay?"

She was scaring the lawn boy.

She was completely decimated. And not even the thought of crushing garden villain number one could perk up her spirits. Sophia glanced at the vegetable plot and all she felt was tired. A bone-deep I'm-never-going-to-get-over-this fatigue. That little thrill, the one at the beginning of spring when the first tender pea shoots broke through the soil, had disappeared. She wondered if it would ever return.

If David were still alive, he would say something like "Pay the kid and get rid of the grubs." She could picture him at the dining room table, with books and papers spread all over the place and his glasses falling down his nose. He'd been completely disinterested in the house and garden. That was her responsibility. He didn't want to know about grubs, or talk about grubs, or think about grubs, unless they had something to do with the sociopolitical climate of medieval Europe.

David probably wouldn't have noticed if their front yard was a pile of dirt.

That made her smile. The thought of David trudging through a pile of dirt to get to the front door, stepping inside, noticing the bottom of his pants covered with muck, and saying, "Where did this come from?"

Sophia laughed. It was a comical thought, and so very David, Mr. Bumbling Absent-Minded Professor.

"Mrs. Brown? So…are we on for the insecticide application?"

She shook her head. "No, I don't think so. I'm going to feed the grubs and skunks this year. They deserve something to eat that isn't poison."

The lawn boy looked at her as though she'd lost her mind. Which she probably had.

✦ ✦ ✦

"Mom. Cady and I found a casting call today. In the paper. And we think you should apply."

Sophia looked up from her plate. She'd been counting rosebuds again. On the edge of the chipped Limoges china. When she glanced at the girls, she was surprised to find them both staring at her intently.

"Casting call? For a film? I don't understand."

Cady smiled. Her sweet, lovely smile. It was crooked. Ever since she was a baby, she'd had that lop-sided grin. Sometimes it looked like a smirk—off-center and full of attitude. But eventually, as the baby grew up and began to speak and take care of her dolls and plants and the other neighborhood children, Sophia realized she didn't have a smirk in her. Just pure, sweet thoughtfulness.

Sophia needed to do a better job of hiding her melancholy. She would rather die than cause her daughters worry. And they were worried.

"It's not for a film. It's for a reality television cooking show. They're looking for amateur cooks. You would be perfect, Mom." Cady pushed a newspaper in front of her.

"I think you should do it. It will get you out of the house. It will be a good distraction." Em bit her lip. Dispensing advice to one's mother was a tricky business.

"It will be an adventure." Cady reached over and squeezed her hand. "You need an adventure. You gotta do it."

"We're not taking no for an answer." Emilia made eye contact with Sophia. Her daughter's gaze blazed with determination.

Sophia laughed. "You two are full of crazy ideas. I couldn't possibly—"

Emilia shook her head. "You could possibly."

"I agree. Why do you think this is crazy?" Cady spooned a large serving of raspberries with chocolate mint sauce onto her plate.

Sophia took a deep breath and tried to gather the energy to respond to their good intentions. "Girls, I couldn't possibly be on television. Look at me. I'm old. I'm haggard. I'm tired."

Emilia raised an eyebrow. "You're forty-seven. You're gorgeous. You need something new and different to energize you. This year has been brutal. You need to find your inspiration again."

How did she know that? How could a twenty-one year-old kid possibly know that?

Sophia picked up the newspaper clipping. A production company was looking for amateur cooks to compete on a new show. The contestants needed basic cooking skills but not professional training or experience. It would take place over a one-week period during the month of August.

"This is insane."

"You know what? That's why you should do it. You need to get out of your rut. Do something insane!" Cady pumped her spoon above her head.

"You're a nut." But Sophia laughed.

Emilia picked up the paper and began to read.

Do you love cooking? Do you enjoy experimenting in the kitchen? Are your dinner parties the most popular event in the neighborhood? Then, WE WANT YOU! Send in an application to the Vermont Culinary Institute. Show us your enthusiasm and your culinary creativity. Finalists must appear on Monday, August 3 for the commencement of filming. MAY THE BEST MAN WIN! See if you have what it takes to be part of our team for A TASTE OF HEAVEN.

"Be brave," Emilia said.

Be brave.

Be brave.

Could you be numb and brave at the same time?

"Carpe diem!" Cady said.

Sophia was creative. But the enthusiasm part might be a problem.

"I don't know..."

"You have no plans for the summer. You have nothing to lose. If you get eliminated on the first day, you come home and we'll figure out Plan B." Emilia, the voice of reason, was not going to let this drop.

"She's not going to lose. She's going to win." Cady shot the lop-sided grin at her mother.

Em shook her head. "It's not about the winning. It's about the experience."

"I know," Cady said. "But she's still going to win. Mom has a kick-ass palate, and she can throw together an incredible meal out of nothing. Even though she tries to hide it, she has a competitive streak a mile long. Remember the 'peony incident' with Mrs. Long?"

Sophia frowned. "There was no incident. Mrs. Long made a big deal out of nothing."

"Says the woman with ten thousand peonies in her garden."

They all laughed.

"Okay, maybe there was a small incident. But there was no way in hell I was going to let a little old lady trounce my peony collection."

"Whatever you say, Mom." Em turned to her sister. "I think you may be right. Mom's going to win."

Cady nodded sagely. "Yep."

Sophia stood and began to clear the table. "I'll think about it."

She was still contemplating the list of requirements—creativity, enthusiasm, competitive spirit. How about the ability to taste?

It might be a wee bit of a problem to participate on a cooking show when everything tasted like cardboard.

But that was something her daughters did not need to know.

Chapter Two

When did your identity as a couple usurp your identity as an individual? Not on your wedding day. The bride was still the center of attention. Not really during the first five years of marriage. You still had your own interests, your own social life. When the children were babies, your identity switched into someone's mother, not someone's wife. But slowly, carefully, persistently, in fits and starts, creeping through your life like a vine, that identity took hold. It put down roots, sent up tender shoots, until they turned tough and woody and only the explosion of an unplanned heart attack could shred them into compost.

And then the fresh-faced bride from years ago was transformed into the melancholy princess, face creased, arms freckled, psyche wounded in strange ways.

Sophia and David had become, Sophia…Sophia, the widow.

Sophia, the lost soul.

And even though it was a pointless task, because nothing could piece together the shredded stems, you still tried to fix it sitting in a trench of soil and earthworms and six-packs of basil seedlings.

You still tried.

"Mom!"

Startled, Sophia glanced up. Her eyes were unfocused. She'd been holding onto a basil plant for possibly ten minutes? She had no idea.

Cady and Emilia peered at her over the edge of the picket fence.

"What are you thinking about? You seemed a million miles away." Emilia hurried into the garden and gently extricated the plant from Sophia's hand.

Cady grabbed a trowel, dug a hole, and popped the seedling into the row. "There. All done. I think you've had enough sun today, Mom. You're losing it."

Emilia and Sophia laughed.

"The sun, huh? Is that why you think I'm losing it?" Sophia kissed her younger daughter on the top of her head, in the nest of dark curls, not unlike her own. But missing the silver slivers.

Cady threw the trowel down. "Time for a change of pace, Mrs. McGregor. You've been gardening like a crazy person. And all you have to show for it is a bunch of muddy boots."

"That's not true!" Sophia answered. "Soon you'll be chomping on tomato bruschetta and singing my horticultural praises."

"Soon you'll be a household name," Emilia said. Her eyes shone with determination.

Sophia turned, anxiety clawing at her stomach. "What have you done, Em?"

"We signed you up."

"For the cooking show," Cady added.

"You wouldn't do it on your own. So we filled in the

application for you. The whole thing." Emilia plucked weeds and tossed them into a pile.

"We even sneaked a photo one day while you were gardening. You look gor-geous!" Cady waggled her eyebrows.

"Do not throw a hissy-fit," Em instructed. She linked her arm through Sophia's and tugged her toward the house. "Time to pack. You passed the initial application part of the contest. You need to be there at eight a.m. tomorrow for filming."

Sophia dug in her heels. Literally, in the muck. And refused to move. "No. Absolutely not. You girls had no right—"

"We had *every* right! Every right! Do you think we're just going to sit here and watch you waste away, and—"

"Cady, calm down." Emilia censured her sister.

Tears poured down Cady's cheeks. "No. I'm tired of pretending everything is okay. While Mom stares into space holding a freakin' basil plant for half an hour."

"Honey, please don't worry."

"Oh, I'm way past worried."

Sophia wasn't used to seeing this expression on her younger daughter's face. She looked world-weary, much too knowing. It was breaking Sophia's heart.

"Mommy."

Oh, hell.

"He's not coming back. And you need to move on. With something new. Something to get you…excited about living again. *Please.* Just try this."

Cady was pleading with her. How could she say no? Even though the thought of this show was a nightmare.

"You told us a long time ago you had a dream of going to culinary school, and opening up your own little place. Remember?" Emilia prompted. "Go have fun. Just think of all the stories you can tell."

"When I was afraid to go on that big sailing trip, you told me to grow a pair." Cady grabbed her mother's hands.

Sophia sighed. "That was completely different."

Cady shook her head. "How? It's exactly the same."

"You're young. Your whole life is ahead of you. I want you to experience everything. My time has come and gone, honey. With or without your father, my days of exploring and sailing off into the ocean are done."

"Bullshit." Emilia's hands shook.

Hell, now she's angry.

"I agree with Em. That is bullshit. It's time to start over, Mom."

Tears leaked down Sophia's face. *Dammit.* "I'm too tired." Her voice was ragged. She was falling.

"I know," Em said. "I know you're tired. You need to find some new energy. Doing the same old thing that you used to do when Dad was alive, it's not helping. Just give this a try."

"What's Plan B?" Sophia asked. She was afraid of the answer. Ship her off to an island? Electroshock therapy? Plastic surgery?

Cady laughed. "Don't look so scared. Plan B is a trip around the world. Actually, we're planning to do Plan B with you no matter what happens with Plan A. We thought we could use some of Dad's insurance money and travel to all the places we've dreamed of."

They were all crying now. And sitting in the dirt. They hadn't even made it to the porch.

"Okay. You girls are killing me."

Cady and Emilia's faces broke out into enormous grins. Shit-eating grins.

"Don't get cocky. I'll probably only last forty-five minutes."

"Bull. And shit. You're gonna win the whole damned thing." Cady hugged her mother.

"We'll help you pack." Emilia said.

"Damn you, girls. This is insane."

Maybe she needed insane.

Chapter Three

The competitors were sizing each other up. Seated at a long wooden table, Sophia scratched in the answers on her paperwork. Women and men, young and old, with callused hands and tattooed forearms and crazy eyes surrounded the table sneaking looks at everyone else. Looks filled with insecurity. Over-confidence. Forced indifference. Even youthful foolishness. Good God, some of these people didn't look old enough to drive!

She completed the confidentiality agreement and handed it to an intern who was cavity-inducing perky.

"Thank you, Mrs…Brown." The girl nodded. "Please put on your apron and join the contestants in Room Fourteen. Right down the hall. Here's your entrance ticket."

Sophia slid the faded King Arthur Bakery apron over her T-shirt and calico sarong skirt. She'd decided comfortable was more important than looking stylish for the camera. The girls had laughed at her this morning.

"You're trying to undermine your chances," Em said with startling insight.

"I have no idea what you're talking about," she answered.

Cady giggled. "Em's right. You think by wearing your old clothes, they'll overlook you. Not happening. No matter what you wear, you still look stunning."

Sophia shrugged. "You mean old. I still look old." She twisted long dark hair into a bun and secured it with a comb.

Emilia slid a slender arm around Sophia's waist. "You look elegant. You look mysterious. You look intelligent. Every wrinkle, every line, every freckle is beautiful."

Sophia swallowed painfully and glanced away.

"Don't ding your own chances, Mom. Give it a go."

And so here she was, against her better judgment, standing in front of Room Fourteen. She pushed open the door and became instantly aware of hostility and tension.

"Nowhere on that announcement did it say amateurs and professionals working together! *No. Where.*" A giant thundered his words in a thick Scottish accent. "I traveled halfway across the globe for a chance to compete in a *professional* contest. Not with a bunch of no-name amateurs. You insult every one of us who has struggled in culinary school and crawled our way to the top in this industry."

A crew of interns and producers surrounded the man, attempting to placate his temper.

"Mr. Adamson, I assure you this concept will be a huge hit for the network—"

"I don't care about your bloody network. I care about the quality of the competition."

A small man with sweat on his forehead tapped his clipboard. "We kept the details of this competition a secret on purpose. We didn't want anyone else to jump on this ship before we launched our show."

"Your ship is going to sink." The Scottish giant glared at the crew.

The little man shook his head. "I don't think so. This is totally new and innovative, and I think it's going to work like a charm. If you don't think you can hack it—"

The giant leaned down until his gaze was eye-level with the producer. "Can *I* hack it? That's not the question, is it? The question is what will happen when a wee amateur tries to keep up with me?"

Eyes blazing, the Scot surveyed the room. His gaze landed on Sophia. He sneered. "Just look at her. Like a scared puppy. There is no way these play-at-home mummies can keep up with the big boys."

Sophia lifted one eyebrow. That's all. She kept her face relaxed, neutral, void of emotion.

This cool, calm response to melodrama had driven David crazy. She stepped forward and handed the producer her ticket and paperwork.

He scanned the application and smiled at her. "Mrs. Brown, good to meet you. I'm Harold Smith." He held out a soft manicured hand and shook with enthusiasm. "You're the local gal, I remember. With the impressive garden."

"It's nice to meet you, Mr. Smith."

"Your name came up quite a bit when we spoke with local nurseries and farm stands. They said you've been instrumental in helping introduce new winter-hardy varieties of herbs in the area."

"Yes, well—"

"Excuse me, sir," The giant grated, his burr pronounced and trailing. "If you're quite done flirting with the pretty gardener, we have more pressing matters to discuss."

Mr. Smith looked perturbed. But Sophia could tell the giant would make good television. He was larger than life. He was loud. He was angry. With a thick red beard, shiny bald head, and an attitude enormous enough to bully all the other contestants. He had a presence that was both off-putting and charismatic at the same time.

He took a step, just one step to the right, and blocked her view of Mr. Smith.

One step.

And suddenly she wanted to win.

She wanted to beat the giant. She wanted to beat everyone.

She wanted to sneak into the game like a quiet little mouse and crush them all.

She was tired of being overlooked. She was tired of being someone's wife. Good little wife, with the sweet little garden and charming parties and so self-sacrificing.

No one would see her coming. She looked non-threatening. She looked like a doll. That's what David used to say. Like a china doll with big dark eyes and porcelain skin, dotted with freckles like cinnamon on a bun.

Sophia angled her shoulder and slid past the giant. She felt the heat of his body as she brushed past him. "Mr. Smith? Where would you like me to go?" She completely ignored the giant. As though he didn't exist. As though he were of no consequence.

Mr. Smith's face lit up when he saw her. "Of course! Let me show you." He turned back to the giant. "We'll finish this conversation later." And just like that, the giant was dismissed.

She made the mistake of glancing up at the Scot's face as they left the group. Eyes as blue as indigo caught her gaze. With a promise of retribution.

A single expression popped into her head. One of Cady's favorites.

Bring it.

Ø Ø Ø

"Welcome to *A Taste of Heaven*! This is so exciting!" Mr. Smith surveyed the contestants with undisguised glee in his eyes.

Sophia wondered why he was so enthusiastic. She had

a sinking feeling it had something to do with the giant's concerns.

"As you all know, the Creativity Channel is hosting this competition, which will be aired next year. The Vermont Culinary Institute was gracious enough to offer their lovely facility for our taping. That means we get to film in this gorgeous landscape and reap the benefits of fresh produce, dairy, and other local products for the show. We are *thrilled!*" Mr. Smith wiped the sweat from his brow with a white linen handkerchief. "We put out a casting call for professional chefs from all over the world. We have chefs from the UK, Europe, Asia, Canada, and the United States. Young and old, some fresh out of culinary school, some with years of experience. So *exciting!*"

Sophia wondered how many times Mr. Smith would say *exciting.*

"We also put out a casting call for amateur cooks. Regular folks who enjoy cooking for their families, have a bit of natural talent, but no formal training." He waggled his eyebrows. "Now for the *surprise!*"

Here we go.

"We lied to all of you." He winked for the camera. "This is not a professional contest. This is not an amateur contest. *A Taste of Heaven* will be pairing one professional chef with one amateur for the duration of the competition. The two contestants must produce a perfectly complementary dish for the judges, and each of them must prepare some part of the meal completely on their own. How quickly can a partnership be formed? Is it possible for two strangers to become a cohesive creative team in just one week? We're not looking for the amateur to be merely a sous-chef or assistant for the professional. We are looking for a true blending of ideas and culinary vision, a genuine partnership. This is the premise for *A Taste of Heaven.* Isn't that *delicious?*"

"Was that a rhetorical question?" The booming voice,

thick with sarcasm, came from the giant himself.

"Ha! I'm sure you can rise to the challenge, Mr. Adamson. We are starting with sixteen contestants. After each challenge, one or more pairs will be eliminated from the competition. The final winners will receive fifty thousand dollars."

Sophia glanced at the pack of chefs. It was obvious that some of them were pros. They looked insulted, angry, and pompous. Others were slovenly and slouched. Some appeared eager, some curious, some like they were ready to sharpen the knives in front of them and behind their backs. She scanned the group and wondered if she could work with any of these people. Time would tell.

"I hope you're all ready to cook, because our first challenge is about to begin. Follow me, please." Mr. Smith led them down a hallway and banged open a set of double doors with a dramatic flourish.

The contestants gasped. It was a dream kitchen, gleaming with stainless steel and top-of-the-line appliances. The set married old-fashioned Vermont craftsmanship—birch stools, exposed beams, and a dark hardwood floor—with modern technology. Shelves were fully stocked with blenders and grinders and pressure cookers. Copper pots dangled above their heads, strung up with brass chains. Sophia thought of her mismatched teacups at home, the scuffed mortar-and-pestle, her favorite dented soup pot she'd received as a wedding gift twenty-three years ago. She sighed. This kitchen was nothing short of spectacular.

Next to her she heard a long, low whistle. "Jesus Christ." The Scot turned to her and shook his head. "You bloody Americans don't know the meaning of simplicity. Everything has to be over-the-top. Brand new and shi-*nee*."

He drew out the last word with such contempt, Sophia couldn't resist responding.

She adopted her well-respected Scottish accent and leaned close to him. "We like…*shi-nee.*"

He raised one eyebrow at her comment and his nostrils flared.

"How do you like your new kitchen? Isn't it gorgeous? The Creativity Channel and the sponsors for *A Taste of Heaven* have generously donated this new facility to the Vermont Culinary Institute." Mr. Smith's white teeth flashed under the lights. "But something's missing, right?"

A petite French woman yelled out, "*Oui.* Where is the food?"

"Where indeed?" Smith answered. "Let's go check the courtyard, shall we?" His oxford shoes clicked on the floor as he approached the back of the room. A dark curtain hung across the entire wall. He turned to the cameras and smiled. "I present…the courtyard!" The curtain slid away to reveal a wall of glass. Several production workers slid the transparent panels along the tracks until the entire room opened up onto a massive outdoor kitchen.

The contestants filed outside, stunned by the extravagance. It doubled the size of their workspace. Stovetops and grills were set into brick counters. Refrigerators were tucked safely under a canvas canopy. And best of all—most thrilling of all—was a lush, vibrant perennial border that surrounded the entire kitchen, filled with edible plants, herbs, and flowers. Bright orange nasturtiums nodded in the afternoon sunshine, tender peas twined about a chicken wire fence. Bees hovered over patches of fuzzy thyme. Sophia laughed out loud. This was utterly delightful.

"Your dream-come-true, Miss Garden Fairy?" The Scot's thick arms crossed his chest. He looked utterly disinterested.

"There are fully-stocked pantries inside, as well. But the outdoor facility takes advantage of our beautiful Vermont landscape. Edibles in the garden." Mr. Smith pointed to glass-fronted coolers. "Local cheeses and other dairy products." He sauntered over to the canopied area and the cameras followed him. Baskets of fresh produce lined the tables. "We have locally farmed proteins, fruits, and vegetables. Honey. Maple syrup. Anything and everything you can imagine." He took a perfectly ripe strawberry from one of the boxes and popped it into his mouth. "This competition is not just about using your technical skill and your culinary education. This competition is about using natural products that are available right now. Seasonal, fresh, inspirational. We look forward to an exciting week, where a range of backgrounds and expertise will showcase these wonderful Vermont offerings."

Mr. Smith approached the contestants and nodded in solidarity. As though they were all on the same team. All working together.

At least for the camera.

"Time to jump right in!" For a moment, his face took on a manic glow. "Our first challenge will be the *only* challenge you do *on your own*. Each of you is responsible for an *amuse-bouche*. For our viewers at home who are not familiar with this term, I'll elaborate. *Amuse-bouche* is French for 'mouth amuser.' It's just one bite to whet the appetite, to showcase a cook's culinary vision and approach. Our judges—who will be introduced shortly—will rank their favorites, from best to last. And this will determine the teams. The winners will get to do a blind tasting and choose the chef they believe will pair the best with their own style of cooking. *You* get to be the judges today as well. Unfortunately, we will also be saying good-bye to the lowest ranked pair. The bottom two—the pro and amateur with the lowest scores—will be eliminated today, leaving us with fourteen pairs for the duration of the contest. The lucky seven."

The cameras panned in closer to Mr. Smith's face. His bowtie was just a smidge crooked. Sophia wondered if the editors would fix that later.

"Just. One. Bite. What will you make? It should showcase your talent, your technical skill, your point of view as a chef. It should also showcase the bounty of Vermont." The camera swung back to the contestants—jittery, tense, practically bouncing on the balls of their feet.

"Are you ready? You have one hour to prepare the best bite of your life."

In a moment of spontaneous and unscripted release, the contestants shouted, "Yes!"

Sophia nodded.

The Scot grumbled something under his breath.

Mr. Smith pulled a little flag from a basket on one of the tables. It was white, with the outline of a puffy cloud in sky-blue. The logo *A TASTE OF HEAVEN* was artfully inscribed inside the cloud. He raised the flag above his head. Sophia saw his Adam's apple bob up and down, one time. And then the producer yelled, "Go!"

The chefs sprang to action.

Except Sophia.

And the Scot.

Sophia was frozen. She heard the songbirds chirping and felt the warm sunshine on her face. It was one of those stunning Vermont days, when the sky was so blue and far away, it offered both comfort and bittersweet beauty. She watched the other contestants greedily snatch up grass-fed beef and dirt-clumped vegetables and organic chickens strung up by strands of coarse string.

One perfect bite.

She knew what she should do. The judges wanted a complex sauce. An extraordinary protein, expertly prepared. An array of textures.

One perfect bite.

Tart. And sweet. Like her life.

She smiled to herself. No one, absolutely no one, ever made a dessert for the *amuse-bouche*. Dessert was the kiss of death in a cooking competition. Dessert was the red-headed stepchild. Dessert was never the star of the show. Just the end of the show. And usually a hideous disappointment.

The Scot turned to her and bellowed. She'd forgotten he was still there. He rushed toward the kitchen.

May the best man win.

Chapter Four

C hop.
Crush.
Strain.
Grate.
Squeeze.
Bubble and stir, bubble and stir.
Whip, mix.
Press. Gentle, gentle. Watch for cracks.
Drizzle.
Wander in the garden. Tamp down hysterical laughter.
Bump. Cringe at sharp profanity.
Time ticking, distant voices.
Taste…nothing. Still nothing. Pray.
Assemble, paint, and balance.
Lift your head as the last ten seconds tick by.
A sea of eager faces.
And once again, the blue of a Vermont sky, pulling you back
to earth.

Mingled with the scents of garlic and onion and the pungent tang of herbs was the smell of sweat—the anxiety of the contestants as three judges faced them in the kitchen.

The dishes were lined up on a long table, free of labels. This was a blind judging, after all. Sixteen little plates. Could you pour your heart and soul into one bite? Define who you are, who you were, who you wish to be?

She had no business being here, not without a sense of taste. How could she possibly compete? Damn Cady and Em. This was all their fault. Two contestants were going home today. If she made it back home by seven o'clock, she could stop by the liquor store and get a bottle of Cab.

Tonight would be a food-free dinner. Just Cabernet in her yellow Depression glass goblet. Listening to crickets and frogs in her garden. She sighed. That scenario didn't sound as appealing as it once had.

A quiet Chinese woman to Sophia's left made an odd choking noise. Sophia glanced at her and saw sweat on her forehead and a tremble in her hands. Sophia had the strangest impulse to touch those shaking hands and whisper it would be all right. The realization that this type of event was not as it seemed on television was beginning to creep into her consciousness.

"Time to meet our judges!" Mr. Smith's voice boomed in the kitchen. "In keeping with our amateur-professional concept for *A Taste of Heaven*, we have decided to include both professional culinary experts as well as an enthusiastic amateur in our judging panel."

This announcement was met with a giggle from one of the judges. Sophia heard the Scot whisper *"Jesus H. Christ"* under his breath. He rolled the "r" for a good five seconds, and Sophia smiled to herself.

"First we have Mr. Jonathan Rutgers, owner and head chef at *Pioneer*, master of American cuisine, James Beard

Award-winner, CIA-educated. Rutgers is fascinated by the melting pot that makes up American culture, and his cuisine reflects that."

The older gentleman nodded without smiling. His hands were clasped tightly behind his back. He wore faded blue jeans and sneakers with a traditional white chef's apron. He looked like somebody's grandfather. He looked like he had no sense of humor.

"Next up is the uber-popular Tarquin Bailey, our representative from the UK. Classically French-trained, now immersed in cutting edge cuisine. His restaurant, *Wind Chimes*, has won countless awards, and his television show, *Impress Me*, has just been re-signed for its fourth season. Chef Bailey is always opinionated, always entertaining."

Sophia also knew that Tarquin Bailey was the first black chef in Britain to win the coveted Celtic Culinary Award.

Bailey smirked at the contestants and sent a jaunty little wave to everyone. His "costume" was flamboyant and designed to attract attention—tight peg-legged pants, a crisp white shirt, a navy blue bowtie. "So very nice to see all of you today. I can hardly wait to taste your creations." His British accent was buttery soft, but his eyes were sharp. As he scanned the room, Sophia was sure the judging had already begun. How would she stack up?

"Finally, we have our 'amateur' representative."

Another giggle.

"Jenny Curtis, popular blogger who runs the site *Dress Up Your Dinner*, will be joining us this season. She is the quintessential American food blogger, in touch with her fans daily via social media. She has her finger on the pulse of the amateur cook. Please offer a warm welcome to Jenny!"

The contestants clapped politely, and Jenny smiled hard enough to crack her pancake make-up. Sophia knew she was being petty, but her fast assessment was...fake tan, fake boobs, fake hair-color. This woman would be judging her?

She was doomed.

"We're *doomed.*" The Scot hissed it under his breath and Sophia turned to him in stunned amazement. "She…is… fucking…giggling."

"I was just thinking the same thing. *Doomed.*"

"You'd better hope that Jenny likes flowers, little garden fairy." The Scot's gaze remained straight ahead.

"Time for our critique to begin. Jonathan, Tarquin, and Jenny will be tasting your *amuse-bouches* and ranking their favorites. Here we go!" Mr. Smith wiped his forehead with another clean linen handkerchief. He stepped aside as the judges moved to the table.

They whispered and nodded and laughed. Spoons dipped into ramekins, and plates were lifted and inspected. Jonathan speared his food with a knife like a mountain man. He looked the part with his white beard and weathered face and large, hardened hands. Jenny popped morsels into her mouth and then bit her lip. Sophia had no doubt this was a practiced gesture. Sexy. For the camera. And Tarquin Bailey was all business. In spite of his flashy clothes and celebrity personality, he seemed completely focused on the food. In fact, much to Jenny's irritation, he seemed to be ignoring the other judges completely.

After an interminably long period, they finished.

To her right, the Scot stood completely still, like a rabbit facing a predator. Unsure of where to move, what to do. The Chinese woman on her left tapped her foot in a rhythmic beat. Tap, tap, pause, tap, tap. Shaggy black hair hung over her eyes, masking her thoughts. But the nervous foot tap gave her away.

Sophia scanned the plates and felt completely overwhelmed. Those plates showcased techniques she knew nothing about in calculated displays that elevated a piece of food into a work of art. Her simple way of cooking suddenly seemed vastly inferior.

Mr. Smith clapped his hands. "What a delicious feast! So much variety, so much creativity…"

"And a few duds as well," Tarquin interjected.

Jenny and Jonathan nodded.

"Shall we start with those? The bottom of the barrel? Everyone gave it their best effort, but some didn't quite cut it." Mr. Smith turned to Jonathan. "Which *amuse-bouche* failed in your expert opinion?"

As Jonathan began to enumerate the myriad ways the contestants failed, Sophia wondered if this was how a beauty queen felt as the names got called. Were you just good enough, were you the cream of the crop, were you lacking? She always felt sick for the women in those pageants. They must feel so vulnerable, balanced in stiletto heels and covered only with the tiniest of bikinis. Facing the firing squad almost naked. Were these chefs any better? The ones whose names were announced and criticized were not all good sports. Some argued. Others shot off sarcastic comments. Some questioned the judges' palates. The remaining contestants released a sigh of relief as the two eliminated chefs were escorted from the set.

Sophia, the Scot, and her Chinese neighbor were still standing.

"Well, now for the fun part!" Jenny giggled. "The food we liked the best. Sure, I didn't go to culinary school like my two buddies over here—"

Sophia noticed Jonathan Rutgers cringe.

"—but I know what tastes good. And we had some *big* surprises today, didn't we fellas?"

"We certainly did." Jonathan raked his gaze over the remaining contestants. His hands were still clasped behind his back.

Sophia wondered if a bottle of Cab would lighten him up.

"Not only surprises, but some truly remarkable food. I can't wait to match the dishes with each of you. Especially my favorites." Tarquin winked.

"Let's start with the best. Tarquin, what impressed you most today?" Mr. Smith asked.

"One hour is not a lot of time to create complex flavors. Some of these bites were spectacular, rich, and satisfying. I'm amazed the chefs could accomplish this so quickly. But for me, I always look for contrast. Tart and sweet, soft and hard, rich and light. And presentation is important."

Jenny the blogger clapped her hands. "Oh, I agree! That's why my blog is called *Dress Up Your Dinner*. Folks who just slop some food on a plate are missing a big part of the dining experience. People need to put the same amount of energy into creating a gorgeous dish as they do with their make-up and accessories and shoes. It's all about the details." She smiled for the camera, flashing the brightest, whitest teeth Sophia had ever seen.

Jonathan Rutgers looked like he was about to choke on his tongue.

Mr. Smith nodded at Jenny's inane observation. "And Jonathan, what are your thoughts about this first challenge?"

"I like simple. Simple flavors, taking the fresh bounty around us and using it in inspired ways. Adding a bit of surprise."

"So, judges, what was your favorite dish?" The producer stepped back so the cameras could pan over the long table.

Tarquin answered.

"A crisp almond tart."

Sophia's heart began to pound.

"Smooth lemony custard. Light as air."

She clenched the edge of her worktable.

"Only one person chose the boysenberries as an ingredient today. They were ripe, juicy, bursting with flavor. But somewhat difficult to wrestle with in terms of tartness. This contestant made a truly inspired syrup, infused with basil... and lemon thyme, I think." Jonathan shrugged. "I can't wait to find out how this syrup was created."

Sophia started to sway.

The blogger smiled. "I love lemon. It's bright. It's sunny.

30

But I don't have a big sweet tooth. This dish was not too sweet. It was lovely."

"And best of all," Tarquin interrupted, "a little surprise under the tart. Hidden. Using the organic bittersweet Vermont chocolate we provided. Well played."

"And the flowers!" Jenny sighed. "This plate captures the very essence of summer. Sprinkled with flower petals."

The Scot tensed beside her. "You have got to be *fucking* kidding me…"

The judges lifted her plate.

Her plate.

Her plate.

My plate!

"Take a breath, lassie. Or you're gonna fall over and wreck the big reveal." The Scot's rich voice snapped her out of her trance.

She slowly inhaled.

"It's a rare day when a non-savory offering catches our attention like this," Tarquin said. "But this single bite was phenomenal. Tart and sweet, crunchy and smooth, making the Vermont local ingredients shine."

"So who is Number Three? A professional chef or an amateur?" Mr. Smith swung his gaze over the contestants.

Sophia took a shaky step forward. She was keenly aware of thirteen sets of eyes glued to her back. "An amateur. A very shocked amateur."

Mr. Smith grinned. "Well, isn't that exciting? An amateur won our first contest! Judges, this is Sophia Brown."

Tarquin shook her hand. "An amateur bested the competition. I love it!"

Jonathan introduced himself. "A courageous first step. You took a big chance preparing a non-savory dish. Keep it up, Ms. Brown. So *how* did you make the syrup, if you don't mind me asking?"

"Or snatching the recipe, right?" Tarquin joked.

Jonathan actually blushed! Sophia wanted to laugh out loud, but she composed herself.

"I used orange basil and lemon thyme. I wanted to bring out some citrusy notes in the syrup."

Jonathan patted her hand. "Very nice."

Jenny gave her an awkward hug. "Oh, I just love the pretty flowers. Your dish was so charming. Very *well-dressed*."

The forced intimacy was uncomfortable. And Sophia was squirming under the intense scrutiny of her fellow contestants. She could feel their hostility. The back of her neck turned hot.

"So what inspired you to make a dessert for your *amuse-bouche*? How did you approach this challenge? And were you intimidated by the thought of competing with professionals?" Jonathan asked.

"I just decided…"…*What did you decide Sophia? To be brave? To be daring? To be carefree? To crawl out of your hole, that safe place, that quiet place, that place with no taste? What did you decide?* "…to try something different. To be honest, I didn't think about the master chefs cooking around me. There's no way I can compete with their experience. I just created something I knew my daughters would love to eat."

"Well, it certainly worked." Jonathan shot her a small smile.

Sophia had the odd sensation her answer had pleased him somehow.

"What flowers did you use for a garnish?" Tarquin asked. "Just curious. I'll let the contestants know right now I insist that everything on your plate is edible. And that includes flowers." He was no longer winking at Sophia.

"Johnny Jump-Ups. *Viola tricolor*. Completely edible, with a mild, slightly sweet flavor. I use them all the time in salads." Sophia's voice was soft, but firm. She had no intention of bowing under pressure from the judges. Not about plants. They could criticize her cooking all day long, but no one could trip up her botanical knowledge.

Tarquin nodded. "Excellent. I look forward to tasting more of your inspired creations, Sophia." His British accent had become more pronounced over the last thirty minutes. There was more to Chef Bailey than the actor mugging for the camera.

Mr. Smith motioned for Sophia to move closer to the table. The crew rearranged the dishes into two groups. "And now our winner gets to pick her partner. These are the professionals' selections. You need to choose your favorite. Choose wisely. Someone whose cooking style will complement your own."

Sophia glanced at the remaining contestants with trepidation.

They stared back, not bothering to hide a host of emotions. Animosity, doubt, impatience, vulnerability.

Time for the moment of truth.

Would she be able to taste their creations?

 Chapter
Five

Seven plates.

Green and brown. Red and orange. Saucy.

Deconstructed gazpacho with chili peppers. Heat, but little else.

A delicate dumpling with sesame and ginger. Overwhelmed by salt.

Vegetable bruschetta. The crunch of asparagus. Texture, but no taste.

Was this a futile undertaking? Should she bow out now? Concede defeat? She looked over her shoulder and caught the Scot's gaze.

Taunting her.

She kept going.

Sweet and salty. Bitter. Muted, but there. When would her sense of taste kick back in? Hell, it better be soon. Clunky and heavy. Underseasoned and much too subtle. Was it her defective taste buds, or really a lack of flavor? She wasn't sure.

Some daring bites, and others that tried too hard to

impress. Sophia liked simple. The dishes with foams and gels were not her first choice. Someone else could partner with those chefs.

One after another, she tasted and moved on.

One after another, she waited for something to jump off the table and shake her.

Two plates left.

Second to the last, and it was brown. And dull. No color. No texture. She lifted a piece of sourdough bruschetta slathered with seafood and a light-colored sauce. She bit carefully into the creation.

Her mouth exploded with flavor. Prawns and lobster swimming in the most delectable sauce. Buttery and layered, with whisky and leeks and onions and simple herbs.

Sophia moaned.

There was more than just one bite on this plate. Thank God. Not strictly a true *amuse-bouche*, but Sophia didn't care.

Was it bad form to lick the plate in a cooking competition? This drab little plate had miraculously fixed her taste bud deficiency. Unbelievable. The moment had just shifted from black-and-white to color, like a scene from the *Wizard of Oz*. Who had created this dish? Someone with a sophisticated palate but no eye for visual presentation.

The last plate beckoned, but she already knew it was a lost cause. There was no way it could best that seafood stew. It was a lovely crepe, packed with grilled eggplant and goat cheese. And now that Sophia's taste had been awakened from hibernation, she was able to enjoy every bite.

But it still wasn't enough to out-shine the prawns.

Those prawns sang to her, and they needed her. They demanded color and brightness. The sauce was bold and rich. That plate clamored for the balance of her garden. She could imagine a prickly little salad to offer texture and bite, to complement that exquisite sauce.

Those prawns needed her.

She turned to the contestants and hid her trembling hands behind her back.

"Quite a range of offerings, right?" Mr. Smith nodded at her encouragingly. "Any favorites?"

"Yes. I definitely have a favorite."

"Don't keep us in suspense, Sophia! Who will be your partner?" Jenny squeezed her arm.

Sophia gently extricated herself from the overly-enthusiastic blogger and stepped to the table. She walked by the dumplings and the crepe and the deconstructed gazpacho. She stopped in front of the drab little plate. Brown, humdrum little plate that had awakened her senses and demanded attention. "My favorite dish was the prawns and lobster in this luscious sauce."

"Ahhhh. The American fell for the seductive whisky sauce." Tarquin said.

"Nice choice, Sophia. The sauce was divine," Jonathan added.

"And not a flower in sight." The Scot's voice rumbled over the set, dripping with disdain.

"Oh dear Lord. Is that Elliott Adamson's dish? Good luck to you," Mr. Smith whispered to Sophia.

She looked over the sea of faces—the tense Chinese woman, the bohemian hipster with his perfectly creased bandana, the French professional with her tight smile. The Scot wore a deceptively lazy expression, but his hands were fisted at his sides.

Oh my God. Not him. Anyone but him!

"Mr. Adamson, is this your dish?" Jonathan asked.

"Yes. I'm the proud owner of the seductive sauce. Who knew I would snag a bonny American garden sprite?"

That elicited a sprinkle of tense laughter.

"Can you tell us about your plate? Your inspiration?" Jonathan returned his hands behind his back and waited for the Scot's response.

"Of course. It's my take on a traditional Scottish recipe, prawns in whisky sauce. Typically it's cooked in a ramekin, but for the *amuse-bouche* I served it on sourdough toast. My inspiration today is the same as every day. The rich history of Scottish cuisine."

His look dared anyone to argue with him. Dared *her* to argue. Those startling indigo eyes found her staring at him, and he glared back.

"Do Scottish people care about presentation, Mr. Adamson?" Jenny seemed oblivious to Elliott's contemptuous mood.

He turned to the American blogger with a face as still as stone and grunted.

"Well, the sauce was beautiful, and clearly impressed our amateur winner, Mrs. Brown. Sophia, please join your partner while we announce the next finalist." Mr. Smith gently nudged her in the right direction.

Toward the scowling, angry Scot.

They stood, side by side, neither speaking nor acknowledging the other. The tension rolled off Elliott Adamson in furious waves. She pretended to watch the rest of the competition, but her attention was focused solely on the man to her right. What had she done? Inadvertently chosen the worst possible partner? His food was exquisite, but how could she work with a man who refused to even look at her?

Doomed.

The old Sophia—the "David and Sophia" Sophia—would have nodded and smiled and played along, quiet and accommodating, always appropriate and thoughtful and kind.

But David was gone. And perhaps it was time for that old Sophia to die a gracious death, too. Even though she'd been dragging it on, somewhere in purgatory for the last twelve months.

This man standing next to her would expect submission. This man would expect her to comply with his demands. But *she* was the one who had won today. And no one here knew David. No one here knew "David and Sophia."

This was a chance for a fresh start.

The hell with *doomed.*

Finally, they were all paired up. A few of the professionals were gracious with the amateurs, but most of them could barely conceal their contempt. And the amateurs looked completely overwhelmed. Sophia wasn't sure this concept was going to work. It would be tough for the amateurs to exert any sort of creative control in the kitchen with a group of egotistical pros.

The man standing next to her was the worst of the bunch.

Mr. Smith beamed at the finalists. "What an exciting show this will be! For the duration of the competition, you will be living in the Vermont Culinary Institute dormitories. Each day for the remaining week we'll be introducing a new challenge. Some will be held here at the new facility. And some will take place during 'field trips' at different locations in Vermont. Our first paired challenge is tomorrow morning. So rest up and get ready. The judges and I can't wait to taste your next *heavenly* creations."

Champagne was poured for the remaining contestants, and they all raised their glasses to toast the commencement of *A Taste of Heaven.*

* * *

The second she placed her glass on the table, a massive paw snagged her hand and dragged her away from the set. Out of the kitchen. Down the hallway. Outside the building. And Chef Elliott Adamson didn't stop hauling her until they reached the parking lot.

"What are you doing?" Sophia made sure her voice was calm and detached, but inside her emotions were in turmoil.

"I'm getting to know my new *partner.*" He spat out the

word. "Who knew all I had to do was throw a bunch of flowers on a plate and I could win this illustrious competition?"

"Who knew?"

Elliott's eye twitched at her sarcastic response. "Let's get something straight, Mrs. Brown. I'm a graduate of *Le Cordon Bleu* London. I've been a professional chef for twenty-seven years. I've owned three restaurants in the UK, and I won the *Best New Chef UK* award in 1988." He leaned down until his face was just inches from hers.

She noticed the mole near the edge of his lip, and the salt-and-pepper in his thick red beard.

"I might not know a goddamned thing about flowers, but I know how to cook. You just stay the hell out of my way, and we'll be fine."

She stood silently for a few minutes to give him time to regain his composure. His chest was heaving.

"Why do you think I picked you?"

He scowled. "I have no bloomin' idea. You like lobster? You bloody Americans think lobster is the height of luxury, correct? But when you live in a fishing village, it's just part of the regular seafood offerings. A local bite."

"That's not why."

He clutched her upper arms. Afraid she would run away? Hardly.

"Why don't you tell me? Hmm?"

She stepped closer to him instead of backing off. He wasn't expecting that. His eyes grew wide, and he actually leaned back. There was no way in hell she would tell him the truth. About her husband dying and how the world had dimmed after that. The colors muted and the sounds muffled and the food lost its flavor. How everything turned gray, and even the sunshine failed, even on the sunniest day.

She would never confide these things to Elliott Adamson.

He would never trust her after that. Never listen to her ideas, never respect her opinion. He could never know that she'd lost her sense of taste.

Sophia knew exactly how to get this man's goat and make him listen.

"I loved your dish. It was nothing to look at. In fact, it was probably the ugliest one there."

He tightened his grip.

"But that sauce… It was complex and satisfying and decadent. I loved the layers of flavor—how it started out buttery and rich, and then finished with the whisky and herbs."

His loosened his grip.

"I wanted to lick your plate. That sauce was glorious."

He raised an imperious eyebrow.

"Which you already know. But that's not why I picked you."

Finally he released her, stepped back, and folded his thick arms across his chest. "For God's sake, why?"

"Because we have to cook together. And your prawns need me. That dish needed the texture of a prickly herb salad. It needed some brightness and crunch, some contrast."

"I'm Scottish, Mrs. Brown. We've been cooking these traditional dishes for centuries, and they taste just fine. They don't need a *fucking salad*!"

"Maybe they don't. But I think it would make your dish even better. And more importantly, it would appeal to the judges. They told us what they're looking for. They loved your sauce, but they're looking for more."

The Scot rubbed his face. "Oh, aye, I'm well aware of that. I expected a panel of professionals who are well-versed in all sorts of cuisine. Judges who don't make a gagging noise when someone mentions haggis. But nooooooo….instead I get two Americans, one who has absolutely no goddamned clue what she's talking about. I don't think she has the slightest idea about international cuisine." He closed his eyes. "I'm fuckin' screwed."

"Do you want to win?"

He opened his eyes and glared at her. "More than you could ever imagine. I don't *want* to win. I *have* to win."

"Then you have to decide if you can play by the rules, Mr. Adamson."

"Call me Elliott, little garden sprite. *Partner.*"

"And you can call me Sprite."

Elliott barked with laughter. Some crew members in the parking lot looked up and stared at them. It was hard to ignore this man. He was huge. He was loud. He was infuriating. And strangely enough, Sophia had to admit that something about him was also appealing.

In an overbearing Scottish sort of way.

"All right, Sprite. How are you interpreting the rules of this game?"

Sophia frowned. "Interpreting? The rules are clear. Each of us must prepare part of our dish. Cooking independently. And all of the components must work together as a cohesive meal."

"Uh-huh."

"What?"

"I'm not even a tiny bit convinced you know what you're doing. For Christ's sake, you made *dessert* for our first course! Dessert!"

She crossed her arms. "It won, didn't it?"

"Give me a break. It won because you used local products—which I'm sure makes the sponsors happy—and tossed a bunch of pretty flowers on a plate. Which doesn't indicate to me you have any clue about cooking."

"I beat fifteen other contestants today. That doesn't seem like a fluke to me."

He narrowed his eyes. "Fine. Let's see how tasty that *amuse-bouche* really is. I'm feeling peckish. You know what I'm in the mood for?"

Sophia shook her head.

"Lemon custard. Almond tart. *Boysen*berry sauce."

"I thought you didn't like dessert," she said.

"Nah. I like dessert. And you're about to make me some.

One. Perfect. Bite." He captured her hand and tugged. "Let's go. Back to the kitchen. I wanna see what you're really made of, Mrs. Sophia Brown."

Sophia ripped her hand from his grasp. "I don't have to prove anything to you."

"Yes, you do. You got to taste my food and judge me. I haven't tasted *your* food yet. You've already made some rather large assumptions about how this partnership is going to work." He paused. "Time for me to see what *I* have to work with for the next week. You're going to make me that *amuse-bouche*, and you're going to do it *now*."

The Scot had a point. Fair enough.

She nodded. "All right. Get ready for dessert."

The giant grinned.

Chapter Six

E lliott barged back onto the set as the cleaning crew worked. He ignored them. He ignored the interns and production assistants and gathered the ingredients Sophia listed.

"Obviously we don't need the flowers," she said.

"Obviously."

"Do you ever use vegetables in Scotland? Fresh greens?"

"Garlic is a vegetable."

Sophia laughed.

Elliott pursed his lips. She could tell he wanted to laugh too, but was holding himself back. This was not an auspicious start to their partnership.

He dumped the food onto a worktable. "Get cracking, lassie."

"I have to collect some herbs from the garden. I'll just be a minute."

When she returned to the workroom, she noticed the cleaners and interns sitting on the tables. Watching the show. Watching the giant Scot bully the little American Sprite.

Fabulous.

She pulled a stainless steel bowl close to her. Elliott hovered over her shoulder. She could feel his hot breath on her neck.

She peered over her shoulder. "Do you mind? Backing up a bit?"

"Am I making you nervous?"

"*Back. Up.* Do you want me to do this or not?'

"Aye."

"Then pull up a stool and sit over there."

"With our makeshift audience? Just so you know, I think their money is on you. You're prettier than I am."

She measured flour and salt and began to assemble her tart. The crispy almond cookie was drizzled with a hint of bittersweet chocolate, mounded with lemon custard, and sprinkled with fresh berries and the rich boysenberry syrup that pulled all of the flavors together. Now that she wasn't in a rush against the clock, she took her time, blocking out the onlookers and the Scot and her anxiety. This was the way she truly enjoyed cooking. When you lost yourself in the process, and could savor each step of the journey.

"What are you humming?" The Scot's expression was mildly amused.

"Am I humming?" Sophia gently stirred the syrup on the gas stovetop.

"Aye. You're in the zone now. I'm curious about what music inspires garden sprites."

She stopped for a moment and thought. "I'm singing *Breathe* by Anna Nalick. My daughters like it."

Elliott shook his head. "I don't know this song."

"It's bittersweet, I guess. I've been singing it a lot lately."

"The garden sprite is melancholy? What could possibly make you sad? You seem like you live a charmed life."

Her hand barely trembled as she continued to stir the mixture. "You know nothing about me, Mr. Adamson."

"Why don't you humor me, then?"

"No, thank you."

One of the interns yelled out an encouragement. "Go, Sophia! We want to taste your *amuse-bouche*."

Elliott glared at him. "It's for *me*. Only *me*. The minions don't get a tasting."

She lifted the pot off the stove and set it aside to cool. If it was too hot, it would melt the lemon custard.

"Almost done. We just have to wait for the syrup to cool."

He nodded. "Why don't you sing for me while we're waiting?"

She had no doubt this was all part of some psychological plot to unnerve her. He had an arsenal at his disposal. Physical intimidation. Picking at her melancholy scabs. Questioning her culinary ability.

But she wasn't one of those young, inexperienced kids, looking for validation from the master chef like a puppy dog so eager to please. She was older and wiser and had been around the block a few times. And was quite familiar with the games people play.

And so she sang.

The room got quiet as she sang the lyrics to *Breathe* strong and clear and without hesitation. She sang right to Elliott Adamson, looking into his indigo eyes. Making sure he knew that she would not be swept under the rug or intimidated by his overbearing presence. His eyes widened a fraction as she started, and then she saw a grudging respect creep into his expression. And when she finished the song, she lifted the pot of syrup and poured it over her plate. She watched the dark purple sauce slip over the lemon and pool in the bottom of the saucer.

And because she just couldn't help herself, because she was adept at playing games too, she pulled out the Johnny Jump-Up flowers she'd hidden in her apron pocket and sprinkled them over the plate. Velvet purple petals with golden yellow faces.

She turned to Elliott and handed him the plate. The plate

that represented her life. Sometimes too tart. Moments of sweetness. Bittersweet memories, hidden but still there, always there.

He took the dish from her hand, brushing his callused fingers against her, and whispered, "Well played, Sophia. Well played."

🌢 🌢 🌢

"Go, Sophia!"

"It looks delicious!"

"I want a bite."

The younger crew shouted at Elliott as he examined the dish like a forensic pathologist. He lowered his face to within centimeters of the plate and deeply inhaled. He picked at it with his fork. Picked again.

"Don't play with your food, Elliott."

He smiled without lifting his head. "If you ignore the ridiculous flowers"—he flicked them off the plate—"the custard and sauce smell quite nice."

"Did Mr. Award Winner just give me a compliment? I do believe I'm blushing."

"Don't get cocky. I haven't tasted anything yet."

He took his fork and cut through the whole creation. Balanced a piece of cookie with custard and sauce piled on top of the tines.

"One bite. Here we go." The fork disappeared into his mouth.

Sophia found herself studying his lips. She wondered what it would be like to be kissed by Elliott Adamson. His lips looked firm and decisive. Nestled within a luxurious beard. Would it tickle? Would he be selfish and rushed? Would he be lazy and seductive? She looked down at her feet and tried to concentrate on something else.

"Hmm."

"How'd she do, Elliott?" One of the cleaning crew came

over and peeked at the plate. "Anything left? It sure smells good."

"Hmm."

Sophia lifted a brow.

Elliott lifted one back.

She knew the dessert was good. She'd tasted as she cooked. And now her taste buds were just fine, thank you very much. It was all perfectly balanced. The sweet, the tart, the hint of chocolate, the fruity syrup with herbs and honey.

He took the dish and placed it in the sink, and then gestured to the cleaning crew. "We're done now. You can finish up here." He turned to Sophia and grunted. "I need a drink. Let's go back to the dorm, and we can finish our conversation there. Discuss the rules of the game."

And he walked away.

Was she supposed to follow him? Was she supposed to beg for his approval?

Hell would freeze over before that happened.

He turned and shot her an exasperated look. "For Christ's sake, Sprite. Let's go. We need to have a council of war. Figure out our strategy for this competition. There's a lot at stake. And tomorrow's our first big challenge. What the hell are you waiting for?"

"Your assessment of the *amuse-bouche*? The one you just insisted I prepare for you?" She refused to budge until he said *something*.

He nodded. "You'll do."

He continued walking towards the dorms.

What would it take to get a real compliment from Chef Adamson? She had no idea. But evidently this was as good as it would get today.

She picked up the forgotten flowers. They would make a sweet bouquet.

Chapter Seven

The dorms at the Vermont Culinary Institute were nothing special—not like the luxurious accommodations on some of the other reality cooking shows. Which explained why the cameras were missing in action. No sponsors to please, no appliances to showcase. Stilted laughter floated down the hallway, where the motley crew of cooks huddled around a keg. They were drinking beer and still sizing each other up. Elliott and Sophia arrived to a noisy round of applause.

"Look who showed. Grumpy Scottish Bastard and The Big Winner." A skinny young chef took a swig of his beer and smirked. "The pair to beat."

The French woman held out a hand to Elliott. "*Bon jour*, Monsieur Adamson. Nice to see you again."

Elliott nodded briskly. "Helene. I hear congratulations are in order. You've graduated from being Monage's sous-chef."

She shrugged. "At last. The master is finally slowing down."

"Elliott Adamson. It's been a long time." A tall man approached the two of them. He was fit and fair, very handsome in a classic American way.

Sophia stepped back. It was obvious many of the pros were already acquainted. And the tension levels seemed to rise as Elliott jumped into the fray.

"Baldwin."

The chef laughed. "Still a man of few words, I see. How's your latest project coming along?"

Elliott crossed his arms. "Fine."

"But you're here, aren't you? Must be a reason for that."

The man was goading Elliott, and it was working. His jaw clenched.

"I could ask you the same thing. What are *you* doing here?"

"I'm opening up a third restaurant in Chicago, and I wanted some exposure. There's no better publicity than a reality TV show. Works like a charm." Baldwin took a drag from his beer and adopted a blasé attitude, but Sophia wasn't buying it for a minute.

"Are you still flipping burgers?" Elliott asked.

"Are you still putting haggis on the menu? I wonder what the perky blogger will think about that."

Elliott drew in a long breath and released it. Sophia had the feeling he wanted to clock the chef from Chicago.

"Too bad the international contest they lured us with turned out to have an amateur judge, an American who hasn't been current in decades, and Tarquin. *Christ.*" Elliott closed his eyes.

"I know what you mean. I'm not much into molecular gastronomy. They could have done better with the judges." Chef Baldwin glanced at Sophia. "You lucked out. A sweet little partner who can actually cook."

Sophia was instantly uncomfortable. Baldwin inspected her with undisguised interest, and it had nothing to do with her cooking ability. Elliott took a step to the right and blocked the man's view.

"Aye. Be grateful for small mercies. Who's your partner?"

"Kevin Holt from North Carolina. Amateur, but he knows his barbecue. That could come in handy."

Elliott scoffed. "Barbecue? We're in the middle of Vermont. I don't think barbecue is on the goddamned menu."

"We'll see."

"Hey, Short Chubby Guy! Come 'ere!" The young chef at the end of the hallway tossed beers to several contestants.

Elliott scrubbed a hand over his face. "Who the hell is that? Do we all have nicknames?"

Baldwin laughed. "He's our resident hipster from Portland, Maine. Johnson, I think. I'm Lancelot."

The quiet Chinese woman said, "I'm Shaggy." Her accent was heavy, and she was still tapping her foot in nervous agitation.

"I'm Sophia. Do you have a real name?"

That elicited a small smile. "Yes. Lin Lin."

"You're a professional chef?"

"Yes," she sniffed. "Tossed in with a bunch of amateurs. My partner is a woman named Tammy. From *Texas*. I hope she can cook," Lin Lin added, looking doubtful.

"The amateurs must have some culinary ability, otherwise they wouldn't have been chosen for the competition." Sophia was beginning to get irked with the condescending attitude.

"One would hope. Perhaps showing the contrast between true talent and incompetence is a winning formula for the producers. Who knows?" Lin Lin sipped her beer and stared off into space.

The atmosphere at the makeshift party wavered between awkward tension and manic anticipation. Most of the pros were studiously ignoring the amateurs, too haughty to even bother with superficial conversation. And the amateurs looked scared out of their minds. Sophia needed a drink.

"Elliott, I'm going to grab a beer. Do you want one?"

"I want two. We obviously aren't going to have a quiet, private conversation here. Hurry up and we'll find somewhere else to talk."

She left him scowling at the other chefs and went in search of alcohol.

As Sophia rummaged through a bucket of ice, she wondered if she'd be sleeping alone in one of the dorm rooms or be partnered with another contestant. This was beginning to feel like the worst parts of college—performance anxiety and cramped accommodations.

"I'll take that." Elliott appeared behind her and snatched a beer out of her grasp. "Too bad it's not whisky, but it will do for now. Let's head to the quad and find a quiet spot. I need some fresh air anyway. This place is a dump."

He took her hand and pulled her out of the dorm. Outside the sky was black and star-filled, not in the slightest bit interested in man-made concerns or mounting anxieties. Elliott continued to clutch her hand as he rushed along the uneven sidewalks. Sophia was sure he was completely unaware of that fact. She, however, was not.

For twenty-two years, she'd gotten used to a slender hand, smooth and soft, linked with hers in a mindless way. David would often flex and tighten his fingers sending her some unconscious message. She peered down at her hand clutched by this angry Scottish man and had to suppress a wince. His massive hand was thick and hairy and rough. Elliott's hand yielded no give-and-take. It was all take.

She yanked her hand away. She was perfectly capable of walking without his assistance.

He shot her an amused look as he stopped in front of a bench and gestured for her to sit.

"God. I wish I still smoked." His voice sounded rough.

Sophia raised a brow. "Doesn't smoking dull your sense of taste?"

"Aye. That's why I quit."

"There's more liquor in the dorm."

"Oh, don't worry, I plan to help myself when we get back." His eyes narrowed. "But not too much. We need to be on the ball in the morning." He stood in front of the bench with his arms folded tightly across his chest, towering over her with the haughty attitude of a king assessing the lowliest of servants.

"How much experience do you have?" he barked.

"Cooking experience? I've been cooking for myself since I was a teenager. Nothing too fancy, but I have the basics down."

"Can you make a demi-glace?"

"Yes."

"A red wine reduction?"

"Yes, I do that a lot with my daughters."

"We all know you can make dessert. That might come in handy if we have a sweets contest. I'm not big on baking."

"I can muddle through."

He sniffed. "Muddle my arse. How are your technical skills in the kitchen? Knife skills, sauces, sautéing? Can you make stock for a soup?"

"Of course. What are—?"

He interrupted her. "Fine. That's better than I expected."

"For God's sake, I'm forty-seven years old. I have two grown daughters. I've made soup once or twice in my life. Just because I didn't win a *Best New Chef* award doesn't mean I'm a complete idiot in the kitchen."

Elliott raised an eyebrow. "Well, well, well. Pretty little garden fairy has a wee bit of a temper, does she?"

Sophia ignored the taunt. It was time to learn something about Elliott and his culinary vision. "What sort of dishes do you typically prepare at your restaurant?" She highly doubted he had succumbed to any trendy culinary methods. She couldn't imagine him playing with molecular gastronomy. He seemed firmly entrenched in traditional cooking.

"I prepare Scottish food. Cock-a-Leekie soup, Finnan

Haddie, roast partridge, smoked goose, shepherd's pie. Haggis. Food that is rich and comforting and real. I don't do *gels*."

She nodded. "That's good. I'm not too keen on that stuff either."

He continued as though she hadn't spoken. "My cooking celebrates the lengthy tradition of Scottish cuisine, recipes that are inspired by the land and sea around us. There's no reason to think Scottish dishes are solely for an undiscriminating or unrefined palate. Anyone with a sophisticated culinary education should be able to recognize that."

"Elliott, you don't have to convince me—"

"Furthermore, these dishes don't need flowers or herbs or bits of *green*." He spat out the last word vehemently.

"Are you finished?" she asked quietly.

"Am I *finished*? No. We are at the beginning of our journey together, and it's imperative you and I are on the same page."

She rolled her eyes. "Let me guess. The Elliott Adamson Page."

"Damned straight."

"Don't you want to know what *my* cooking approach is?" she asked.

The look on his face was comical. "No."

"No? Not at all interested? You aren't curious if we're compatible…"

He leaned down and boxed her in with his arms. Lowered his face until it was just inches from hers. "Let's get something perfectly clear. This is the Elliott Adamson Show. I'm the professional chef. I'm the one with the experience. I'm the one who has everything on the line. Not you. I bark orders. You follow them like a good little girl. I make the decisions. You follow my lead. I don't want to hear your opinion. I don't want you making suggestions. I lead. You follow. *Is. That. Clear*?"

Is that clear?

What was clear to Sophia was a cauldron of fire building inside of her. Rushing to the surface like a plume of lava, ready to burst forth, showering the earth. What an insufferable bastard. So cocky and dismissive.

Sophia's days of being a good little girl were over.

She lifted her hand and pushed his chest. He didn't budge. She pushed harder and he stepped back. Sophia adopted a cool, composed facade while inside her emotions were churning. She was shocked by the violence she felt. She wanted to strike Elliott, slap him, wipe the smirk off his face. She took a deep, calming breath and stood. "I'm surprised, Mr. Adamson. I thought you said you wanted to win. But it seems like you'll be disqualified before the contest even gets underway. Either you play by the rules, or you lose. And the rules state that we *both* have to participate. Both of us. The judges will ask us what we made, how we contributed to the dish. I'm perfectly capable of enhancing your vision, but we have to work together. Unless you knock the enormous chip off your shoulder, we'll be done before the first round is over. Decide. *Do you want to win?*"

Sophia had delivered that speech with nary a wobble in her voice. Inside, she was quaking and shocked by this new side of her personality. And perhaps a bit proud of herself as well. This new Sophia. Who would not be cowed.

Elliott turned red. He stared at her in stunned disbelief. *Yes*, she wanted to shout at him. *The garden sprite does have a temper!*

His eyes darted back and forth, an indigo blaze raking over her face. She could see the barely suppressed tension in the tautness of his mouth, the twitch of an eyelid. And she knew he was recalculating this relationship. Reassessing her. Reassessing the situation. Trying to squeeze her into a compartment that was comfortable and predictable. Wondering how he would manage her. Wondering what she was capable of.

He really had no idea.

Did *she*? Did Sophia have any idea what she was truly

capable of? She was about to find out.

Finally, he nodded. "Fine. You have a point."

Breathless, and surprised by his response, she sat back down on the bench. "Instead of towering over me like an irate ogre, why don't you sit and we'll talk. And actually listen to each other."

He reluctantly seated himself next to her. "An irate ogre?" She raised a brow.

He laughed. "You would fit right in with my employees. They all hate my guts."

"I wonder why. Do you charm them with the *I Lead, You Follow* lecture?"

"Yes," he chuckled. "It works much better with them, thankfully, than with my American partner. They're all on board with my rules at Stone Soup."

"Is that the name of your current restaurant? Stone Soup?" she asked.

"Yes. Named by Wife Number Three. Tucked behind a stone wall in North Berwick, near the sea. In a dark, dank, dreary spot that is…well, never mind. The food is flawless."

"Wife Number *Three*? You're kidding, right?"

"I never kid about ex-wives. They're not a laughing matter." He stared off into the night as fireflies began to spark around them.

Three wives? *Dear Lord.* Part of her was not surprised. In spite of his infuriating attitude, something about Elliott Adamson was extremely provocative. That combination of single-minded intensity and rough masculinity was captivating.

She cleared her throat. "I used to read *Stone Soup* to Em and Cady when they were little girls. They loved that book."

"Wife Number Three joked I could make a gourmet dish from anything. A rock. A stick. A piece of coal."

"Does Wife Number Three have a name?" Sophia was curious.

"Wife Number Three is now Ex-Wife. Like Wife Number

Two. And Wife Number One." Are we going to talk about food or yak on about my miserable love life?"

Clearly, the ex-wives were a sore spot for Chef Adamson. "Very well. I'm ready to talk about food, Oh Lord and Master."

He laughed at her sarcasm. "Fine. Tell me about Vermont. The types of products they will throw at us. What can we expect over the next week? I had no idea the contest would be like this. I honestly thought a crew of professional chefs would be tossed into a kitchen and battle it out." He frowned and released a bone-weary sigh.

For the first time Sophia saw the tiniest bit of vulnerability in Chef Adamson's swagger. "I can tell the premise for this competition has thrown you for a loop, Elliott. But I assure you I'm a competent cook."

"We'll see about that. In the meantime, educate me about Vermont."

Sophia told him about fresh cream from the local dairy and grass-fed beef from the farm one town over. Honey from the Akins bee skeps, syrup tapped at the local university. The organic turkey farm that raised plump birds racing for their lives the day before Thanksgiving, and then turned into a ghost town once the holiday was over. She told him about every local Vermont product she could imagine that *A Taste of Heaven* might include in the competition. He was silent, mulling over every word. And she could see the gears and wheels in his brain clicking and turning and creating as he assimilated the possibilities. When she'd finished, he continued to sit next to her, lost in thought, silent and brooding.

Finally, he spoke. "Very well. We play by the rules. But I'm still captain of the team."

"Team Grumpy Scottish Bastard?"

He started out chuckling, but soon his booming laugh was echoing across the green, streaming up into the open windows of the dormitory, and floating on the nighttime breeze into the Vermont starry sky. "Grumpy, indeed. Time for bed."

She walked back to the dorm, wondering what wheels she had set into motion by choosing the prawns in whisky sauce.

It was a sobering thought.

Chapter Eight

The dorm room looked like a prison cell.

A Taste of Heaven may have invested in a brand new courtyard kitchen for the Vermont Culinary Institute, but they certainly hadn't invested a dime in the dormitories. Skinny mattresses topped the rusty bed frames. The walls were dingy and plain. Pipes lined the ceiling, occasionally hissing and clanging like an angry wraith.

Sophia found her duffle bag on top of a mattress.

Lin Lin lounged on the other bed.

"Hello again. Looks like we're roommates…at least for now. Until someone goes home." Beneath the shaggy mop of bangs, one dark eye glared at her.

Already exhausted by her Scottish partner, Sophia had no intention of continuing the hostility with her roommate. "I'm glad we're together. Where are you from?"

Lin Lin brushed the bangs from her eyes and sat up straighter. "From Vancouver. I have a restaurant there. I heard you're local."

Sophia sat down on her bed and winced as it creaked. Hopefully she wouldn't fall through the floor tonight. "Yes, I live about fifteen minutes from here. I traveled to Vancouver years ago with my late husband. We loved it. Such a gorgeous city."

Lin Lin nodded. "Uh huh. Good food city. Do you think these judges will like Asian-inspired cuisine? Tarquin leans more toward Indian inspiration, and Rutgers is old school, I think. The blogger…eh. Who knows? She seems ridiculous." She began to tap her foot on the faded bedspread. "This competition is not what I expected."

Sophia smiled. "I don't think it's what anyone expected. That's the whole point. The producers are forcing all of us into an uncomfortable situation. I have a feeling this show will be more about teamwork and less about the food."

Lin Lin shook her head. "No, you're wrong. It is *always* about the food. The teamwork part is a wrench in well-planned strategies. That is all. The food will win the game." Her one visible eye gleamed, and the tapping stopped. "Hopefully Tammy will not be as clumsy as she seems tomorrow."

"Tammy from Texas?"

Lin Lin nodded. "And she stutters. She is a nervous wreck."

"I'm sure everyone will calm down once the cooking starts."

Lin Lin shot her a doubtful look and turned on her side. "I'm reading before I sleep…about Vermont products and resources. I want to be ready tomorrow. Please turn the lights out in thirty minutes."

Sophia sighed. She had no doubt that all of the "amateurs" were being bossed around right now.

She changed into sweatpants and a T-shirt and slipped under the thin blanket. Was this another tactic to keep the contestants rattled? For the first time, Sophia wondered how much of this contest was a psychological experiment by the producers. Were they trying to ramp up the tension for the show? She understood they needed drama for entertainment, but she was planning to be as prepared as possible for tomorrow. And it had nothing to do with reviewing cooking techniques.

She pulled out her laptop and typed in *ELLIOTT ADAMSON*.

An hour later she was huddled beneath the shabby blanket so the light from her computer would not disturb her roommate. Lin Lin snored quietly from her corner of the room and was grinding her teeth. Still nervous, even in sleep.

Sophia poured over photos and menus and reviews. And wedding announcements. Elliott with Wife Number One—small and dark and shy. With Wife Number Two—golden and fair. And with Wife Number Three—stocky, joyless, holding a pot spilling over with claws.

Early photos revealed a lean, beardless Elliott, all smiles and swagger, surrounded by friends in a cramped kitchen. Eventually the man became heavier, harder, grim. Dark circles began to appear under his eyes. A thick red beard cropped up on his face like a shield, but not enough to mask his solemn expression. The last several years of photos were telling. No more smiles for the camera, no more wives by his side. He looked haggard, and bleak, and all alone.

She found snippets of reviews. Tourists thrilled to find authentic Scottish cuisine. Tourists complaining about appalling service. Customers who raved about impeccable food. Restaurant critics shocked by a dreary, dark atmosphere. There were just as many disgruntled comments about his establishments as positive.

Sophia began to inspect the menus, one at a time, analyzing each dish. She searched the Internet for information about Scottish cooking, the most popular traditional dishes and their history and preparation. By the time a purple sunrise began to creep into the window, she had collected some perplexing information about her new partner.

Elliott Adamson was an enigma.

He was obsessed with food. But apparently clueless about the rest of the details involved in running a successful restaurant. He barreled through projects as frequently as wives. When one restaurant faltered, he left it—and the wife—and started fresh.

How had a man filled with so much talent failed to launch?

The answer was there, hidden somewhere behind the clenched jaw and stubborn mouth and eyes as blue as the sky in North Berwick.

Sophia had no idea what was holding him back. But she was ready to move forward. And this big, brooding, bullheaded man was standing in her way.

This competition was her chance for a fresh start. And if she had to bully the Scot to get there, so be it.

✎ ✎ ✎

"Rise and shine!" An intern grinned cheerfully as she pushed open the dorm room door. "We're having an early challenge today."

Lin Lin groaned from her bed. Sophia pushed herself up on one elbow and glanced at her watch. Five a.m. *Oh my God.* She'd had scarcely an hour to sleep.

"What's the challenge?" Sophia's voice croaked.

"You'll find out soon enough!" The P.A. chuckled at the two of them. "Grab a quick cup of coffee and meet me outside in half an hour. The van is leaving for our challenge location."

The intern disappeared.

Lin Lin growled.

Sophia rolled out of bed and hurried to dress. She pulled on a pair of cargo pants, a white T-shirt, and a cotton sweater. Vermont mornings were always cool, even in the summer time. She'd peel off the layers later in the day. She clipped her hair and slid on her most comfortable sport clogs. She had no·

idea what was coming up, but her appearance was the least of her concerns.

Thirty minutes later, a cavalcade of vans bumped along the back roads. Elliott was in another vehicle and hadn't bothered to acknowledge her in any way. Fine. Soon enough they'd be forced to interact. God help her.

It didn't take long to arrive at their destination. When they pulled into the gates for Pumpkin Hill Farm, Sophia's heart lightened. This was a wonderful location and a real working farm, not just for show like some of the touristy spots. It also boasted a lovely restaurant and gourmet market. She and David had visited often with the girls when they were little. One of her favorite family portraits was the four of them perched on the stone wall at the entrance. David held Cady in his arms, her face covered with candied apple and dirt. Emilia, who was always the fastidious child, had a corduroy shirt buttoned up to her chin, and two perfect braids decorated with Halloween ribbon. Sophia's face was in profile, watching her family, smiling at her family.

Loving her family.

And now as she watched the television crew mount cameras and lights around the farm, she looked for ghosts along the wall. But all she found were candy wrappers and chipmunk holes, lichens, and chipped chunks of granite.

"Sprite!" Elliott's voice boomed over the set. He stood next to the café entrance and looked about as welcoming as a tree trunk.

"Good morning, Chef Adamson."

He inspected her, top to bottom, and grunted. "Did you sleep at all last night?"

She sighed. "An hour or so. Why? How bad are the circles under my eyes?"

Elliott shook his head. "You look like a strong breeze will blow you over. Are you ready to cook?"

"I'm ready."

"We'll see. Just remember what we talked about last night."

"I will. The part about working together."

"And me being team captain."

There was an edge to his voice that made Sophia nervous.

They entered the kitchen area to find it bustling with crew members and contestants. The chefs were rounded up and herded outside for the filming to commence. They stood in front of the main barn to introduce the show.

Mr. Smith waved to the contestants. Today he wore a gray suit and pink tie. Sophia wondered if he realized how out-of-place he appeared while standing in front of the pig stalls on a farm.

"Are you ready for Challenge Number One? Breakfast is the perfect way to start the day…and to start our Vermont challenges. We are currently guests at Pumpkin Hill Farm, a lovely little farm with fresh dairy, livestock, and produce. Pumpkin Hill employs fifty-nine hard-working farmhands who have already been up for hours. So here's your first challenge. You and your partner must prepare a family-style platter to serve at least ten people. You have three hours and will be working in the café kitchen. We are looking for breakfast fare. Something satisfying that takes advantage of the bounty around us—something creative and unique and inspiring. Don't forget. You and your partner must each plan and contribute part of the dish. Who's ready to cook?"

Sophia turned slightly to Elliott, ready to discuss their options, but he ignored her.

"We're ready! We're ready!" Short Chubby Guy pumped his arm in the air.

The rest of the contestants laughed.

"Excellent! Your time starts now!" Mr. Smith waved the *Taste of Heaven* flag.

The contestants sprinted away.

"Elliott!" Sophia yelled after him but he wasn't interested in conversing. "Elliott, please."

He almost knocked over a gangly chef with acne scars on

his cheeks. The chefs fought for rations of bacon and thick slabs of ham. They pushed and shoved and jockeyed for position, trying to hoard the best ingredients. Sophia saw more than one egg fall to the ground and splatter.

She clenched her fists in exasperation. *To hell with him.* She raced to the farm stand and began to gather fresh mushrooms still covered with soil, ripe tomatoes, and tiny purple potatoes. She also gathered bins of fresh citrus fruits.

When she got back to their station Elliott was chopping furiously.

"Elliott. We need to talk."

"I need to cook."

"Yes, so do I. Do you want to discuss our menu for today?"

"Not really."

"We could play twenty questions, or you could just tell me what you're making."

"I'm making a traditional Scottish breakfast. Black pudding, tattie scones, and homemade sausages. With broiled tomatoes and fried mushrooms. The farmers will love it. No damned way they're gonna eat bacon *foam.*"

"You're not making black pudding." Sophia blanched. She remembered the ingredients for black pudding...mainly blood and fat and oatmeal.

"I am."

"Elliott, think about your audience. The judges. Jenny, the blogger. Do you honestly think she's going to like black pudding?"

"I am *not* going to compromise my cooking to accommodate that ridiculous woman. Any well-seasoned international chef should be able to appreciate this dish." He continued dicing onions.

Sophia was astounded by his speed and accuracy. And horrified by the containers of blood and suet.

"I have an idea." Sophia rinsed her fruits and vegetables in the sink behind them.

"No."

"Listen to me—"

"No."

"Elliott! Listen to me!" She heard the tremor in her voice. Her legendary patience and calm demeanor had deserted her.

"Why don't you make a pretty little fruit salad we can squeeze on the side of our platter, Sprite?"

His hands flew over the cutting board.

"Elliott, I spent some time researching Scottish food last night. Instead of tattie scones, why don't we grill the purple potatoes and serve them with fresh rosemary? And the traditional sautéed mushrooms and broiled tomatoes could be lightly grilled instead. I'll season them with herbs from the garden. Just to lighten things up a bit."

His hands stilled, mid-chop. His eyes flicked up. "Really?"

She swallowed nervously. "Really." Her voice was steady.

"No. We make them the *right* way."

She forged ahead, ignoring his anger. "I can also make a sauce…"

"Just make the fruit salad, Sophia. I have a lot to do. Don't bother me again."

And just like that, she was dismissed.

They had attracted the notice of the other contestants, and Sophia cringed at their smug smiles. They were all thinking the same thing. *Thank God I wasn't paired with Elliott Adamson.* They thought she'd made a fatal error when she chose him as a partner. Had she? No longer the pair to beat, but the pair who would sabotage themselves?

She took a deep breath and began to slice the mushrooms. The black pudding would be a hard sell. But she was sure her vegetable sides would work with his rich dishes. Even if she had to physically fight him at the end, she would get her vision on that platter. Sophia knew in her heart it would work.

They labored side-by-side, not speaking. Other contestants laughed and teased. Some argued. Some cried. Sophia heard the splatter of oil, the crash of pans. From time to time she tasted his food. The sausage was delicious, seasoned with ginger and spices. His sides were all buttery and rich—the mushrooms sautéed in butter, the tattie scones cooked in butter. She tried the black pudding with trepidation. It wasn't her favorite item, but it wasn't awful. It tasted a bit like liverwurst mixed with oatmeal. All of his dishes were rich and heavy. She had to lighten up their menu.

Her vegetables looked beautiful—red and yellow tomatoes, grilled Portobello mushrooms, purple potatoes. Colorful, bright, bursting with flavor. She prepared an orange marmalade, another Scottish specialty, and paired it with crispy challah toast. Cady and Em would have loved that part. The fruit salad was all citrus and lemon basil. The sauce fruity and tart.

"Ten minutes! Ten minutes!" Short Chubby Guy announced as he dashed across the kitchen area.

She watched from the periphery of her vision as Elliott chose a brown platter for his brown food.

"No. Not that one. Think about the visual." She crouched down and pulled out a blue-glazed platter, probably made at one of the local potter's sheds.

A tic on Elliott's cheek danced in anger. "Fine. We'll use the pretty plate. I couldn't care less about that."

"I know," Sophia answered.

"Just what is that supposed to mean?" Elliott placed slices of his black pudding on the dish, next to plump sausages and fried mushrooms. He drizzled sauce on the side of the plate. There was no room for anything else.

"It means that you ignore the visual. Elliott, there is no room on that platter for my food."

He scowled. "Just toss some of the fruit on the side. It will be fine."

She edged closer to him. So close she could see the sweat glistening on the hair of his forearms.

"I thought you told me you wanted to win. *Had* to win."

"I plan to. This meal is perfect."

"This meal will get us disqualified, and we'll both be going home. Today."

"Just play along. Put your fruit on the—"

She pushed Elliott out of the way and removed his mushrooms and the tattie scones, spooning them onto another plate. She cut the pudding in half to make more room for her vegetables.

"What the fuck do you think you're doing?" His eyes glittered dangerously.

"Making sure we aren't disqualified." She placed her vegetables next to the black pudding.

"No!" Elliott's voice boomed as swept her food off the platter.

The kitchen froze. The chefs stopped plating and talking and stared at the mess on the floor. Sophia's face burned with embarrassment.

Elliott ignored them all. He calmly took his mushrooms and slid them back onto the platter. Sophia could hear the blood rushing in her ears, feel the tightness in her chest.

Did it matter?

How hard you worked, how much you wanted it?

In the end, did it matter? There was another plan, one you couldn't anticipate. One you couldn't predict.

Did you really have any control? Over the outcome? Over this outcome? Or were you nothing more than a pile of discarded mushrooms, brown and crushed on a dirty kitchen floor?

Short Chubby Guy shot them a nervous look as he announced, "Two minutes."

Sophia stepped in front of Elliott, blocking his access to the food.

It mattered.

She was more. This time. She would be more.

She had officially reached her limit with Grumpy Scottish Bastard.

"You *coward*. You should have told me you had no intention of playing by the rules. I would have asked for a different partner. One with less talent but more competitive spirit. One with every intention of playing to win instead of undermining our chances." Her voice broke. She was close to hyperventilating.

Elliott's nostrils flared. "Don't you dare to fucking psychoanalyze me. You don't know a bloody thing about me or my life."

"I know you just sabotaged our chances for this competition. That's all I need to know." Sophia untied her apron and flung it onto the table.

"Wait." His chest heaved. For the first time he glanced at her work area. "What did you make?"

"Grilled potatoes with rosemary, grill-roasted cherry tomatoes and Portobello mushrooms. I made orange marmalade with challah toast and a citrus fruit salad. And a fruity sauce to complement your savory one." She tried to catch her breath. "I promise you these things will all work together—a fresh twist on a hearty Scottish breakfast."

"One minute!" A deep southern accent shouted out the warning.

"You made real marmalade? From scratch?" Elliott looked shocked.

"Yes. I found a recipe last night while I was researching Scottish food."

Elliott closed his eyes. "Hell. Keep my tattie scones. Use your tomatoes, mushrooms, and the rest of it. *Do it!*" His fists were clutched so tight, his knuckles turned white.

Her hands trembled as she scraped the fried mushrooms off the plate. Thank God she had prepared extra food. Sophia took her remaining vegetables and arranged them on one side of the platter, the fruit on another, the toast with pots of fragrant marmalade nestled on another edge.

The platter looked divine. Colorful, balanced.

She felt the hot brush of his beard against the side of her face as he whispered furiously into her ear. "This better goddamned work."

She shivered uncontrollably. All of the stress and exhaustion had finally caught up with her. "It will work. Trust me, Elliott."

He growled into her ear.

"Time's up. Utensils down!" Mr. Smith beamed at the contestants as he swept his gaze over the array of platters.

She had forgotten her fruity sauce. *Damn.*

Servers lifted the platters and carried them to a banquet table set up outside, under a bright Vermont sky and framed by a charming red barn. This would make for good television. The display was simple—plain white dishes and bouquets of burgundy dahlias. The laborers began to congregate at the table, and the judges introduced themselves and settled everyone into their spots.

The chefs were a mess. Sweaty, exhausted, hyped up with anxiety. They huddled to the side of the set, watching with nervous apprehension as the farmers tasted their food. Sophia wiped clammy hands on her apron and looked around her. None of the contestants were smiling.

An elbow slid into her right side. "I'll bet you're regretting your choice of partners right now." Michael Baldwin pressed up against her and chuckled.

It made Sophia's skin crawl.

She could feel Elliott tense on her left.

"We all knew right away who made the Scottish dish. He's the most predictable bastard on the planet. And the most infuriating. You'll be pulling out those gorgeous black curls before the end of the week."

Sophia refused to look in his direction or respond to his observation. She was most certainly having reservations, but she had faith that Elliott would come around.

Please, Elliott. Come around.

"Too bad you didn't pick Baldwin as your partner, Sophia. You'd be flipping burgers and curling French fries. Baldwin's specialty is *Crap American Food*. He's extremely talented at that." Elliott glared at Chef Baldwin over Sophia's head.

"Shhh! They are calling our names!" Helene, the French chef, waved a hand at the feuding men.

The two bottom pairs were called first. Sophia's body relaxed each time she heard a name called, and it was not her own. One of the pairs was eliminated and left in a cloud of disappointment.

Mr. Smith leaned over the banquet table and gestured to Tarquin. "Would you like to announce your favorite pair first?"

Tarquin nodded. "I certainly would. This was a most delicious breakfast. If I had these platters to choose from I would forgo my usual cup of coffee and indulge. My favorite meal today was prepared by Helene and Nathan. The fresh Vermont ingredients really shone with their preparation. Well played."

Helene and Nathan—a.k.a. Short Chubby Guy from Oregon, hugged each other awkwardly and walked to the judging area.

"Could you please tell me who created which part of your dish?" Mr. Smith asked the finalists.

Helene answered. "Of course. I made the Gruyère cheese soufflé and the grilled ham with apricot sauce. Nathan prepared the yogurt parfaits with fruit compote."

"Nathan, how'd it go with this first challenge?"

"Good. I think I managed okay." His eyes were wild and he looked slightly shell-shocked.

"Did you get a chance to taste Helene's food?"

"Yeah." He nodded vigorously. "She's good."

The other contestants laughed at the understatement.

Jenny clapped her hands together. "My favorite dish was an American specialty. Buckwheat pancakes with a trio of toppings…classic maple syrup tapped right here at the farm, a blackberry sauce with mint, and a delicious maple walnut butter. And the bacon-Brussels sprouts side was crispy and salty and delicious. Congratulations to Michael and Kevin."

Chef Baldwin shot Elliott a smug smile as he and Kevin shook hands with the judges.

Elliott countered with an insult. "Pancakes and syrup. How original."

Mr. Smith patted Kevin on the back. "What part of this dish did you cook, Mr. Holt?"

Poor Kevin was shaking. Sophia felt awful for him.

"I made the bacon and Brussels sprouts. That's one thing we're good at in North Carolina. Frying up the bacon. And I helped to flip a couple of pancakes, too."

Everyone laughed, including Michael. Sophia wondered to herself if that was considered an acceptable contribution to the dish. Evidently it was, since Mr. Smith nodded encouragingly.

Elliott reached for Sophia and squeezed her hand so hard she winced. She was torn between frustration and empathy for this man. Somehow she had to get through to him. If they'd been working together the entire time, their dish would have been the one to beat. She was sure of it.

Chef Rutgers took a sip of coffee before announcing his finalist pair. Elliott could barely contain himself. "My favorite was somewhat unconventional. Not everyone likes black pudding, but I happen to like it very much. This platter took very rich dishes that are old-fashioned and well-loved in the UK and paired them with some fresher, lighter sides. I especially loved the homemade marmalade. I'm a sucker for good marmalade."

"*Fuck. Me.*" Elliott's words would need to be censored out by the editors.

Sophia sagged in relief.

"Chef Adamson and Chef Brown. Nicely done. You two are an unexpected pairing. I like it."

Jonathan began to ask them about their contributions,

and Sophia was relieved she had more than just *fruit salad* as a response.

"Tell us about your inspiration, Elliott," Jonathan asked.

"This is based on a classic Scottish breakfast. I made homemade pork sausages with ginger, nutmeg, and sage, black pudding with pork blood and suet, and tattie scones, a traditional Scottish side. Mr. Smith asked for hearty and satisfying. I made hearty and satisfying."

"Don't you mean *we* made hearty and satisfying?" Jonathan said.

Elliott forced a smile. "Of course. *We.*"

"Aren't Scottish people worried about fat and cholesterol?" Jenny asked.

Elliott glared at the blogger.

Sophia placed her hand on his arm and whispered, "*No.*"

"You took a chance with the black pudding, Chef Adamson. I'm not a huge fan. But the sausage you made is possibly the best I've ever tasted." Tarquin smiled.

Elliott relaxed slightly.

"And Sophia, what was your contribution?" Jenny asked. Sophia noticed the blogger's perky, happy appearance wasn't holding up so well under the Vermont sunshine. She had tight fine lines next to her eyes and acne under the make-up. And the look she gave to Elliott was cold as ice.

"I decided to do a lighter twist on some of the traditional Scottish sides. I grilled the vegetables and made the orange marmalade and the citrus salad. My daughters love that fruit salad, especially with the lemon basil."

"I liked your part of the dish best of all. The bright flavors of the fruits and vegetables. Very refreshing." Jenny turned to Elliott. "So, Chef Adamson, how did the two of you blend your dishes on the platter? Did you taste your partner's food?"

Elliott froze. Sophia—and everyone else on the set—was well aware of the tension between them as they cooked. Damn Jenny. She was putting him on the spot deliberately.

"I did not taste her food," Elliott answered. He cleared

his throat awkwardly. "I assumed since she won the contest yesterday that the woman can cook."

Jenny shook her head, clearly not impressed with that answer. "And Sophia, how about you? What did you think about Elliott's black pudding? And why are you preparing Scottish food? You're American."

Sophia could feel the heat from Elliott's body next to her. He felt like a furnace. There they stood, under a blazing Vermont sun, being scrutinized and prepped for certain failure.

To hell with that.

"I tasted Elliott's food as we cooked this morning. His traditional Scottish dishes were rich and satisfying. I thought some lighter sides would be a nice contrast and balance the breakfast. Black pudding isn't my favorite food, but I thought it was perfect for someone who needs a hearty meal." She glanced at the table of farmers, some of them friendly faces she knew from previous trips. Those smiles spurred her on. "I'm not Scottish, but my partner is. This contest is about blending our two styles. So our platter showcased both of our approaches to cooking—traditional Scottish fare and my love of fresh fruits and vegetables."

Jenny looked disappointed. If she'd expected Sophia to fold under her criticism, she'd underestimated her.

Tarquin nodded in Sophia's direction. "You and Elliott may join the other finalists."

Elliott refused to glance her way. Embarrassed by being put on the spot? She had no idea. He took her hand and pulled her to the finalist area.

Tarquin, Jenny, and Jonathan stood next to Mr. Smith who held a miniature *Taste of Heaven* flag.

"This is so exciting! Our first winning pair! Okay, judges, who will it be?" Mr. Smith waved the flag and winked for the camera.

Tarquin stepped forward and took the flag from the

producer. "Today's winner made a classic brunch sing. Sometimes the tried-and-true favorites pack in the most flavor. And the judges were very pleased to see how this pair utilized the locally farmed maple syrup, one of the stellar products from the state of Vermont. Congratulations to Chef Michael Baldwin and Amateur Chef Kevin Holt." He handed the flag to a flustered Kevin who waved it over his head as the other chefs clapped politely.

It may have been Sophia's imagination, but the applause from the other contestants felt lukewarm at best.

And it definitely was not her imagination that Elliott looked ready to throttle the winners.

"Stand down, Elliott."

"Pancakes. And syrup. Pancakes and syrup." Elliott kept repeating the same thing over and over again.

"It's okay. We're still here. And we were one of the three finalists in this round. That's a good thing."

"A good thing. Uh-huh. Time for a chat, Ms. Brown."

And for the second time in twenty-four hours, Elliott Adamson grabbed Sophia's hand and dragged her off for a lecture. Dragged her like a rag doll.

She was seriously getting tired of it.

Chapter Nine

Elliott pulled Sophia behind the chicken coop and released her. The chickens were less than thrilled with their visitors. Cherry red feathers floated in the air as the poultry squawked and darted around their legs.

"You told me to trust you." He spat the words at her.

"Yes, I did. It's unfortunate that we were still plating one second before time was called—"

"Oh, *no*. Do not blame me."

"Blame you for what? We were one of three finalist pairs."

"We didn't win!" he shouted.

Sophia finally realized that Elliott was not just disappointed, he was absolutely furious.

"We didn't win? What did you expect? We were lucky we weren't on the bottom today. You ignored me until the last *twenty seconds* of the contest. You made black pudding which is probably despised by ninety five percent of the world's population."

"Not in Scotland."

"But we're not in *Scotland*, Elliott."

"You forgot your *fruity* sauce."

Sophia blew out a frustrated breath. "I know. I'm disappointed about that."

"No matter what the contest rules say, *I* am in charge. You know nothing."

Sophia rolled her eyes. "You are such a snob."

"Hmm. Maybe for good reason."

"Reason being…?"

"I'm a trained professional chef. You are not."

"No, I'm not. But I'm smart enough to realize that just throwing a garnish on the side of the plate isn't going to cut it for this contest. Our cooking needs to blend together seamlessly. We can do this."

He barked out a laugh. "God, you're cocky. You actually think you can cook as well as I?"

She shook her head. "Of course not. It would be lovely if you could give me some pointers and suggestions. Instead of ignoring me the whole time!" Sophia heard the shrill tone of her voice and forced herself to relax. She never lost her temper. What was it about this man?

"If you're unhappy with this team, you have no one to blame but yourself. You chose *me*, remember? Now you're stuck with me. Quit complaining." Elliott's burr was so thick she could barely understand him.

"I didn't choose *you*. I chose your food. There's a difference. I had no idea that you had prepared that *amuse-bouche*." She glared at her infuriating partner.

"Regretting your choice?" he asked with a sneer.

"No, your food was the best thing I tasted yesterday. You're a talented chef. But you need an attitude adjustment or we're going to lose!" Sophia yelled.

"You tried to replace my tattie scones with your ridiculous little potatoes!" Elliott yelled back.

A couple of chickens ran away in a panic.

"Yes, I did. If everything on that dish had been heavy and rich, the judges would have rejected it. Jenny has a simple palate. Tarquin likes contrast. We have to think outside of the box for this. I wish I'd had time to put my sauce on the platter. Our two sauces would have been excellent side-by-side. The salty rich sauce with the tart and fruity one."

"Funny how folks in Scotland don't need a fruity sauce to eat their fucking breakfast. Isn't it funny how that works?" Elliott's expression was so arrogant.

Sophia wanted to slug him.

"We're not in Scotland. If you wanted a Scottish contest, then you should have looked for one in Scotland."

He leaned down to her eye level and grabbed her arms. "I didn't want one in Scotland. I wanted an international competition where I could show the world that Scottish food is something special. Something that deserves a second look, and perhaps some accolades, instead of derision."

"You really have something to prove." Sophia wriggled out of his hands.

"Yes, I do."

"Regardless, you have to keep the judges in mind. They are not Scottish, Elliott. Our other 'customers' today, the farmhands, are used to American fare, with lots of locally-grown ingredients. Including fresh vegetables."

Elliott regarded her with stony silence.

"You're welcome, by the way. For saving your butt at judge's table."

He looked away. Sophia refused to let this go. "Jenny was ready to throw you under the bus. Both of us. It's a good thing I tasted your food and could defend our dish. I saved us. Admit it."

Elliott shrugged. "I don't care what that blogger thinks."

"Well you better start caring. She's a judge. And we have to think about the palates of the judging panel and our other guests. My daughters are a good example. They love—"

Elliott threw up his hands. "I don't care about your daughters. I don't care about what they eat, or what you eat, or what you think. I don't care about what your husband eats, or what—"

"My husband is dead!"

The sentence hung in the air, hovering there as its echo ricocheted off the back wall of the chicken coop. Sophia had screamed so loudly, her throat ached. She would be hoarse the next time she spoke.

Elliott was frozen in place. He blinked, but otherwise remained unmoving. As well as unmoved?

They stayed like that, two combatants in the arena, facing each other. Covered with a sheen of sweat and cooking oil. Half of Sophia's hair had slipped from the clip and was now spilling over her face. It blocked her view of Elliott, so she could only see slices of the man, bits of ginger beard, half a mouth, one blazing eye, part of a white apron covered with blood and fingerprints. She shuddered in a shallow and painful breath. Elliott closed his eyes for just a moment, and then he turned and walked away.

Leaving Sophia all alone. And feeling just as empty and hopeless as that day in June when the sky was blue and the birds were singing and her husband was lowered into the earth.

✐ ✐ ✐

"Mrs. Brown, may I speak to you?"

Sophia was curled up on a bench outside of the main barn, hugging her knees. Each of the contestants was being filmed for their "testimonials" with the picturesque farm in the background. She'd already filmed her spot. She'd made a point not to look at the screen, knowing what she'd see. A pale face. A wooden demeanor. Her outburst with Elliott had left her numb. The producer hadn't pushed her too hard, aware of her state-of-mind.

She and Elliott were careful to avoid each other, and the other contestants were keeping their distance as well. As though she were infected with some sort of virus and they were all deathly afraid of contracting it.

Except for Helene, who seemed impervious to anything, including contagious germs.

The French woman pushed Sophia's legs out of the way and sat down.

"You know, Elliott wasn't always so…" She waved her hands in the air. "Such an asshole."

Sophia smiled at her deliberate French accent. *Asshole* never sounded so good.

"You knew him when he was younger?" Sophia couldn't help her curiosity. The photos she'd found on the Internet had made her wonder. Wonder about the man he'd been. The man he'd become.

"*Oui.* We attended some cooking classes together many years ago. I knew him when he was a cocky young chef. Brilliant. Stubborn. Still hopeful."

Sophia frowned. "What happened?"

"Hmm. Life 'appened, as they say. He is a very talented chef. But the man makes horrible choices." Helene pronounced the word "orri-bull."

Sophia smiled. "What sort of choices?"

"Ah, well, wives for one thing. They were never strong enough or dedicated enough for that man. He is driven. And he managed to drive them away." Helene snapped her fingers. "If he had chosen well, they would have stayed. They would have fought for him, for their marriage, for his culinary vision, too." She shook her head and released a long sigh. "And his choices for restaurants! *Mon dieu*, he thinks like a man, *n'est-ce pas*? He cannot see around him, just on the plate in front of him. Customers do not want to smell stinky fish while they eat a gourmet dinner."

"Stinky fish?" Sophia was intrigued.

"*Oui.* He cannot choose good locations. Too small, too

dark, too stinky. If your restaurant is right next door to a fish market, and the waste barrel is outside your front door—"

"Oh my God. That can't be true."

"*Oui.* It is true. And that's not the worst of it."

"I'm afraid to ask what's worse."

"The worst is that Elliott is a big baby. Like most men— but I won't repeat that statement in mixed company." Helene winked. "Anyway, he does not like criticism."

"Oh, I noticed that."

The French chef chuckled. "Yes, if anyone dares to criticize the great Elliott Adamson—customer, wholesaler, restaurant critic—he will explode like a giant volcano." Helene's hands flew into the air as she made amusing explosion sound effects.

"I'm starting to get the picture. Not the best personality for a cooking competition."

"Hmm. Or perhaps the perfect person. Perhaps the show likes the explosions and drama, but has no intention for this man to win? How could a man who prepares black pudding win a show like this?"

"You think they set Elliott up?" Sophia sat straighter on the bench.

"No, not necessarily. I just think that they are probably pleased to see the sweet little American woman with the big bossy Scottish chef. Entertaining, yes?" She raised a brow. "Do you understand?"

Did Sophia understand? That Elliott had tunnel vision— he only saw the food, but no other details. That the television show didn't care about him, but they cared about ratings. Sophia did understand, but she wasn't happy about it.

Helene shrugged her shoulders. "Well. You have your work cut out for you, as they say. He has raw talent, but he must be managed. And he is a big bully. You…" Helene raised a judgmental eyebrow as she assessed Sophia. "You are tiny, but I think you have a steel spine. Is that how you say it? But remember, Elliott is a man. You have to"—Helene made a hitting motion—"clunk him over the head to make him listen. You cannot be polite. You cannot be sweet. You must be a bitch. Do not let that man run you over, the way he did with his wives." She patted Sophia on the knee. "I like you, Mrs. Brown. And I like Elliott, too. Don't give up."

Sophia smiled at the petite French chef. Her face was creamy smooth and clear, her simple clothes meticulous.

"Thank you. I think I needed that pep talk. May I call you Helene? You may call me Sophia."

Helene stood. "You may call me Chef Bertrand."

The two women laughed.

"Very well. Thank you for your advice, Chef Bertrand."

Helene smiled at her and walked away.

Sophia felt like she could sleep for a thousand years. She hoped the testimonials were almost finished and they would be heading back to the dormitories soon.

She needed to rest and regroup. She had a feeling that managing Elliott Adamson would require every bit of energy she could muster.

 Chapter
Ten

Sophia slept. And she dreamt.

Not about her home or garden or the obscure details of her life that cropped up during the darkest hours of the night.

She dreamt about a cauldron over a pit of fire. And she was stirring…stirring. Stirring with a black cast iron ladle, as a primordial soup bubbled. Bits of things bobbed in the muck. Animal parts and organs she would rather not identify. The things were fleshy and brown, tattered and obscene. Even in her dream she barely held back a retch.

Elliott appeared at her side and smiled. "It looks perfect. Ready to serve?"

She groaned.

"Sophia. *Sophia*. Wake up. We need to talk." Strong hands gripped her shoulder and shook her from the nightmare.

"Elliott. Go away. I'm sleeping."

"You're having a nightmare. You're groaning and scowling

in your sleep. Better to wake up and have a cup of coffee. Nice and strong. Try this."

She cracked open an eyelid as he placed a mug on her nightstand.

A pillow sailed through the air and knocked him on his back.

"What are you doing here? Get out! This room is for women only!" Lin Lin screeched at him.

"Ah, Lin Lin. Good morning to ye. Hope you had a refreshing sleep."

"Get out!"

"Elliott, you just can't help yourself, can you? Rubbing everyone the wrong way." Sophia leaned up on one elbow and sighed. Her voice was still scratchy after yesterday's outburst. "Go wait in the hallway. I'll be out in a second." She reached for the coffee and took a sip. "Too bad we aren't having a coffee challenge. This is excellent."

"I'll be waiting for you. Hurry." He waved at Lin Lin as he slammed the door.

Lin Lin shook her finger. "You tell your partner to stay out of our room. He thinks he can do anything he wants to. But that won't work here. Not here."

Sophia nodded. "You're right about that. I'm wondering if he'll realize this is no longer the Elliott Adamson Show. God, I hope so."

She pulled a hooded sweatshirt over her T and faded floral pajama pants and stuffed her feet into a pair of rubber work boots. She cradled the coffee in her hands and enjoyed one quiet sip before facing her partner.

He was waiting in the hallway, leaning against the opposite wall in a rehearsed pose. Feigning indifference.

Sophia didn't buy that for a second.

"Let's go find our favorite bench and have a wee chat, shall we?" He darted his gaze over her attire and smirked. "Sexy. Very sexy. I especially like the pajama pants with the boots."

She ignored him and savored her coffee. "What is so important that you had to wake me before the producers? I needed that sleep."

"Come on. Let's go talk in private."

She followed him along the brick path outside of the dorm until they reached the sitting area. A worn wooden bench was nestled beneath a massive sugar maple. She sat on the far edge of the bench, expecting Elliott to join her. But instead he began to pace. He was wound up tight this morning.

"So." He cleared his throat. "I…ah…apologize for yesterday. I thought about it, what happened. And maybe serving black pudding to the judges and farmers was not such a brilliant idea." He licked his lips. "Although I stand behind any and all traditional Scottish fare. And it peeves me off no end—"

"Stay on track. I've heard this before." Sophia cocked her head. "I find it extremely hard to believe that you came to that conclusion on your own."

He pursed his lips. "Yes, well, Helene may have spoken to me yesterday. The woman isn't shy about offering her opinion."

Sophia laughed in delight. "Helene gave you a dressing down! How fabulous. I wish I'd been there to see that."

He continued and ignored her comment. "Nevertheless, I'm still in charge. And we will continue to focus on basic Scottish food. Enhanced, perhaps, by your flowery little additions. But I'm still the captain."

"Understood. And no more bloody puddings. You will never win over Jenny the Blogger that way. We need her on our side. *All* of the judges."

He nodded. "Yes. You're right. And…I apologize, also, for…"

Sophia sat silently and waited. She had perfected the art of patience in conversation. The waiting…so that people who wanted to be interrupted, people who wanted to be let off the hook, had no recourse but to speak their mind. Even if it was uncomfortable and awkward.

So she waited.

Elliott stroked his beard and sighed. "I am sorry about your husband. I am sorry about…how I spoke to you yesterday. I had no right to speak that way to you."

Sophia remained quiet.

"Don't you have something to say? I just apologized. I *never* apologize."

"Should I be flattered?"

Elliott finally sat down on the bench. "When did he… pass? Your husband?"

"Last year."

"You loved him?"

"Of course."

"There is no *of course*, Sophia. Plenty of people are married who do not love their spouse. Plenty."

"Did you love your wives?"

"I always thought so. The beginning was always fresh and exciting, filled with possibilities." He shrugged. "The end not so cheery. I have a way of making women hate me. I'm sure you find that hard to believe."

She wisely said nothing in response.

Elliott continued, "I apologize. It's obvious you care very much for your family. And I have no business insulting them. Or you." He studied the ground at his feet.

"I do care for my family. Very much. Thank you for apologizing," she answered softly. Elliott looked more than disgruntled. He looked worn out.

"Do you have family?"

"My Uncle Rory. He's eighty-two. It's just the two of us. No more wives. No kids. Just two cranky old men trying to keep the restaurant afloat."

Sophia nudged his foot with her boot. "What's going on with Stone Soup?"

He scrubbed his face with weary hands. "Nothing good, that's for sure."

"Tell me. Is this why you're here? Why you need to win?"

"Aye. I might as well be frank with you. Since we appear to be spilling our guts." He shot her a rueful smile. "I *need* to win this competition. Not for the accolades and attention and popularity, like Mr. Baldwin. I think he fancies he'll be the next celebrity chef."

"What do you need, Elliott?"

"Money. Plain and simple. I need the damned prize money. Stone Soup is about to go under like a sinking ship, and I have no more recourse. The bank won't extend my credit anymore. The investors ran off. Not that I blame them." He shook his head. "This is it. Either I win this damned contest or I'm done. And I don't think I have the fucking energy to start all over again. I've already done that in the past." He released a shaky breath. "This is my last chance."

Elliott Adamson looked exhausted. Sophia knew that look well. She'd been living with it every day for the past year. This big bear of a man, with his short temper and fiery defense of Scotland and its cuisine, hung his head in despair, and Sophia felt the heaviness of his plight weigh down her own soul. And now the two of them were thrown together in this crazy contest, both of them exhausted and vulnerable. He hid his despair behind a wall of anger. She hid hers behind a cool exterior, seemingly unflappable.

What a joke.

She had no real cooking experience, and her sense-of-taste had just barely returned.

Could she do this, fight for both of them? Fight for his restaurant and fight for her future?

Sophia reached for his hand curled around the beat-up wooden slats. "We can do this. We just need to strategize. And be thoughtful about our meals."

He stared at their fingers locked together. His gaze found hers, and he shot her a tight smile. "I'll *try*."

"You can do it, Elliott."

He lifted his hand and ran a rough finger down her cheek. Sophia froze, completely unprepared for the sensation of his work-callused fingertip on her face.

"Look at you. How is it that you look so gorgeous after no sleep, and I look like an old piece of shit? Pretty soon they'll start calling us *Beauty and the Beast*." He cupped her chin. "How old are you, anyway?"

"Forty-seven," she croaked. Desperately hoping her face wasn't flaming. "You?"

"Forty-nine. About to hit the half-century mark. I'd like to get there with my restaurant still intact. You think we can manage to eke out a win today, Sprite?" He released her chin.

She started to breathe again. He had no idea what his touch did to her. And she was planning to keep it that way. He already had too much power in their partnership. The last thing she needed was for him to get an inkling about his physical effect on her.

"I think we can manage it. Just remember, Elliott…"

"What?" He stood and held out his hand.

She braced herself as she took it and stood up next to him. "Just say no to bloody puddings."

Elliott Adamson's booming laugh could be heard over the entire campus square.

Chapter Eleven

"Welcome back to *A Taste of Heaven*! Today's challenge is all about...*beef*!"

The contestants cheered as the camera panned to a long banquet table covered with proteins. Sophia saw roasts and short ribs, steaks of all cuts and sizes, ground beef.

"Loden Farm, which specializes in organic grass fed beef, has been generous enough to share their bounty with us today. Our challenge will take place here at the Vermont Culinary Institute, at our fabulous courtyard kitchen. Our professional-amateur pairs must prepare a dish that utilizes the incredibly fresh and flavorful beef from Loden Farm. They are also welcome to use anything from the pantry or garden. I'm looking forward to tasting some delicious creations at the judging table. What do you think about this challenge, contestants?" Mr. Smith smiled with an overabundance of enthusiasm.

Short Chubby Guy screamed, "Meat!"

The rest of the chefs chuckled, but Sophia could feel the tension rising already.

"Contestants, you have five minutes to discuss your ideas with your partner and then three hours to prepare your food. We'll announce the start time so be ready."

Elliott squinted at the table. "I want that minced beef. We're making cottage pie."

This was new. He was actually discussing their menu before the challenge.

"Elliott, since it's summer maybe we should—"

He scribbled on a miniature notebook. "You collect the potatoes and peas. I'll work on the pie. Maybe we could serve a small salad on the side…" He ripped a page from the notebook and handed it to her. "Get these ingredients for me as soon as time starts."

"Elliott. Listen to me. It's summer time. Don't you think it would be more appropriate to do a lighter dish? Cottage pie is a winter dish. Comfort food on a cold day. Maybe we should grill. How about—"

"Sophia. Stop. This is what I want to cook." He wasn't even looking at her.

Sophia felt her temper rising. "How about grilled steak with mushrooms and sage? I saw a wonderful recipe for that when I was researching Scottish food."

"No."

"Think about the seasonality."

Elliott glanced up and found her gaze. His jaw clenched. "Sophia, let me explain something to you. Cottage pie is a traditional Scottish dish. It was good enough for my mum. Good enough for Da. It's good enough for Uncle Rory. It's been good enough for Scots for hundreds of years. It's good enough for us. And I don't care if it's sunny out or blustery or there's a goddamned tsunami."

Sophia stared into those unblinking indigo eyes and felt her temper ease. "Is this a special family recipe?"

He turned away from her and continued to jot down

notes. "Learned it from my mum. The first thing she taught me to cook. It's a staple on my menu. *All. Year. Long.*"

Sophia nodded. This was important to him. "I understand."

"What are you going to make? You said we have to seamlessly complement each other. Right? How will you do this?" He glared at her. His fingers clutched the pencil so tightly she was afraid it would snap.

He wouldn't back down on the cottage pie, but he was trying to compromise. In his own limited way. *Dear Lord.*

"I guess I'll do a side salad with greens. How about if we put the peas in the salad, instead of the pie?"

"Deconstruct the cottage pie?" He stared at her for a moment and frowned. "I'll keep carrots, mushrooms, onions in the pie. You can add peas and any other *seasonal* green vegetable to your salad. Fair enough?"

That was all the compromise she'd be getting today. And she could see that it cost him.

"Fair enough."

"I'll have to rush to the minced beef. I'm sure Baldwin will be wanting to make his classic burrrr…gers." He sneered.

Sophia wondered how much of this contest was about showcasing the beef, and how much was about outshining Michael Baldwin.

Mr. Smith addressed the chefs. "All right, it's time to collect your ingredients. Who's ready to cook?" Mr. Smith's power tie had red and navy stripes today. "Your time…starts…now!" He whipped the flag through the air.

Elliott raced to get the minced beef. All of the professional chefs jockeyed for position at the protein table, and the amateurs scattered to the pantry, the refrigerator, and the garden. Sophia grabbed a canvas basket at the door as she ran to the courtyard. By the time she'd returned with fresh tomatoes, mushrooms, onions, and herbs, Elliott was already heating oil on the stovetop.

"I got everything from the pantry. Let's start roasting those tomatoes for my puree."

Elliott grabbed the vegetables from her basket and began to dice them at an astonishing speed. Sophia would not have been surprised to see a finger fly through the air. But he was wholly confident with his knife skills.

She took the mushrooms out of the basket and began to prep them for the pie.

"No, like this. It's quicker, more efficient." He took the mushroom from her hand and snapped off the stem so that only the cap remained. Then quickly sliced the mushroom into thin pieces. "See? Faster." He lifted Sophia's right hand, covered it with his own, and popped off the stem. "Got it?"

She stared at his hand touching her own. Elliott's hand, heavy and callused. But no longer so rough and impatient. Gentle, helping her to learn. Finally.

"Thank you," she whispered and pulled another mushroom out of the basket. She snapped off the stem.

He nodded. "Good girl. Can you make some rolls? To go with the pie?"

"Yes, how about rosemary rolls?"

"Excellent. That will go nicely with Vermont butter. I must say I'm impressed with the dairy products in this state."

"My daughter Cady used to sneak spoonfuls of the sweet butter when she was little. We still get heavy cream in the glass bottles from Marshall's Dairy."

"That's one of the reasons I've stayed in North Berwick instead of heading into the city. I love dealing directly with local growers and dairies and fishermen. It makes you feel connected to what you're cooking."

Sophia placed a bowl of mushrooms in front Elliott's workstation. "And I guess it adds to the continuity of creating traditional dishes, when generations of the same families are still fishing or farming for the ingredients, right?"

Elliott glanced up. He wiped his forehead with his sleeve and nodded. "Yes, exactly. You can taste that in the food. Don't let anyone tell you otherwise."

"Two hours and twenty-eight minutes!" Short Chubby Guy announced with glee.

Sophia grabbed a stainless steel bowl. "I'm off to the make the dough. Do you need anything else before I leave?"

"No, I'm good." He huffed out a breath. "Um, thank you."

Sophia bit her lip. "That hurt, didn't it?"

"Like a bitch."

They both laughed.

Two and one half hours later, they had bubbling cottage pies ready in crockery ramekins. Sophia's garden-inspired salad was dressed, and the rosemary rolls were golden brown from the oven. Their dish smelled delicious. The other contestants had burgers and sliced sirloin and ribs and stews. It looked like Kevin Holt and Chef Baldwin had prepared some barbecue, although Sophia thought their platter was too heavy with protein, not enough sides.

Only time would tell what the judges thought.

All of the contestants lined up after the judges had their tasting. Sophia noticed that Elliott refused to make eye contact with her, but he stood close enough to brush elbows every few seconds. He needed the physical connection, even if he wouldn't admit it.

He was obviously nervous as hell.

Tarquin stepped forward and took a low theatrical bow. "Time for the moment of truth. What a fantastic challenge this was for everyone. We had quite a variety of dishes—Asian-inspired, some traditional, some cutting-edge. Some worked wonders with these particular cuts of beef, and unfortunately some failed."

He called two pairs forward, and proceeded to enumerate their deficiencies. It was brutal. Meat overcooked, too tough, too stringy. No flavor. And the kiss of death—no seasoning. The losing pair looked stricken, but left the set without any drama.

Jonathan Rutgers cleared his throat. "Now for the fun

part. The dishes that worked. These were all quite different. Lin Lin and Tammy created ginger beef with crisp garden vegetables that showcased some distinctive, bright flavors. I adored this dish."

Sophia smiled as Lin Lin and Tammy stepped forward. Her roommate looked completely shocked and continued to hide behind a fringe of bangs.

"Go, Shaggy!" Chef Johnson, the hipster from Maine, cheered for his colleague.

Everyone laughed, and even Lin Lin permitted herself a small grin. The two women discussed their inspiration and preparation techniques.

Jenny shook their hands. "I agree with Jonathan. I loved that Asian dish. I also loved the meal that paired perfectly grilled tenderloin with buttery charred lobster. Oh my God! Now that is just the way surf-n-turf should be prepared. Heavenly! And the fresh herb salad with flowers made it such a pretty picture. Congratulations to Brian Johnson and Herman Vergara."

Brian jumped up and down and hugged his sidekick. The two gangly men moved to the front of the room and fist pumped into the air. Sophia envied their youthful exuberance. It was sweet. And now poor Elliott crushed her hand as the final pair was called. She wanted to whisper into his ear and promise him everything would be okay. Why did she care so much about his anxiety? She had no idea.

Tarquin laughed at the hipsters. "Our final favorite meal today took minced beef and turned it into satisfying comfort food. My colleagues thought this dish was too heavy for a sunny August day, but I'm British. We eat meat pie all year long."

Tarquin winked for the camera, and the remaining contestants laughed nervously.

Sophia heard Elliott release a hiss. She laughed out loud and squeezed his hand in solidarity. *Thank God!*

Chef Baldwin whispered "Fuck" under his breath.

"Congrats to Elliott and Sophia, our last pair. They took a traditional Scottish meat pie, and made a luscious meal that really sang with the fresh vegetables from our Vermont garden. Well done."

Elliott pulled Sophia to the line of finalists and nodded to Tarquin as he passed, "Thank you."

"Thank *you*," Tarquin answered. "I haven't had a proper meat pie in months."

Mr. Smith stepped forward, cradling a bottle of wine in his arms. "I'm pleased to offer this spectacular wine from Loden's Vineyard to our winning pair. They'll be able to toast their success tonight! So, Jenny, who are the lucky winners?"

Jenny twisted her head so that the fat blond sausage curls swung into place. Sophia had to fight the urge to roll her eyes.

"Well, Mr. Smith, all the finalists cooked wonderful meals. But Tarquin thought the ginger beef was a little too basic. He's pretty picky about his Asian food, you know?"

Mr. Smith chuckled. "Yes, of course, we know."

Jenny continued. "And the meat pie was tasty, but too heavy for this time of year. Although I'm gonna keep that recipe in mind for next Christmas."

Elliott tensed next to Sophia, and she didn't have the heart to look at him. *Damn. Damn. Damn.*

Not again.

"Our winners today really showcased the beef. It was grilled to perfection, and so tender and delicious. Paired with that delectable grilled lobster, it was a winner for sure. Congratulations to Brian and Herman!"

The two men shouted and ran to Mr. Smith. The producer looked concerned for a moment—probably worried that the hipsters were about to tackle him for that bottle of wine. But they just stood there with their goofy grins as he handed them their prize. Mr. Smith wished them the best of luck for the duration of the contest, and then the camera man yelled, "Cut!"

Sophia was afraid to peek at Elliott. He stood completely

still and quiet at her side. That worried her. Where was the angry bear?

Chef Baldwin stomped off the set, clearly miffed he hadn't finaled for this challenge. He paused in front of Elliott. "Tough luck, Adamson. Beat by surf-n-turf."

Elliott was powerless to ignore the ribbing. "At least my meat pie bested your idiotic American burgers. You're gonna have to step up your game, Baldwin."

Michael shook his head. "At least I have a game. You just keep cooking the same damned things over and over again. When are you going to figure out you need to try something different?"

Elliott had no answer. Sophia waited until everyone else had left and then she gently nudged his arm. "Hey, how about we get—"

"I need some time alone, Sprite." He still refused to make eye contact with her.

She frowned. "Okay, I understand. Maybe later—"

"Time to reflect." His voice was strained, but steady.

"I'll be waiting when you're ready to talk," she said.

Sophia walked away from the wounded bear, hoping his injury wasn't lethal.

Chapter
Twelve

The contestants had the rest of the evening free. A makeshift party cropped up in the dormitory quad, complete with strands of Christmas lights sagging in the weeping willows and folding tables bearing tapas. Free to cook without judgment, all of the chefs had pitched in and prepared delicious mini bites. Sophia grabbed a beer from an ice-packed bucket.

"Hey, Big Winner!" Nathan from Oregon raised his glass to her. "You deserve a medal for sure. What's Adamson got planned for the next meal? Haggis?" He snickered.

Sophia frowned. "Elliott Adamson is a brilliant chef. If you lived in Scotland, you'd be eating haggis, too."

"If I lived in Scotland, but I was competing in the United States, I'd trade the haggis for something with less intestine," he said.

Sophia sighed and walked away. She was not in the mood to defend Elliott. Or discuss haggis. She found Helene seated beneath a willow tree with a few other contestants. They had dragged some chairs under the branches.

"Join us, Sophia. Have you tried Baldwin's sliders? They are quite good."

Sophia raised her beer bottle. "Not yet. I'm starting with the alcoholic portion of the evening."

Helene clucked. "I don't blame you. Today's loss was tough. But I think good for Elliott."

"He did not look too happy," Tammy added as she picked at some food on her plate.

"No. He's trying to jam a square peg into a round hole. And no matter how hard he tries, Jenny the Blogger is not going to champion his cause." Sophia sighed again.

"Jenny the Blogger is an idiot," Nathan said.

"Jenny the Blogger is also a *judge*. We cannot forget that." Helene took a bite of her burger. "This contest is about *strategy*."

"I think this contest is about the *food*," Lin Lin argued. "Not strategy."

"I'm afraid you are wrong, Miss Chin. Take Elliott for example. His cooking is flawless. I'm sure that black pudding he made was a perfect preparation. But if you don't think about your audience, you don't stand a chance here," Helene said.

Michael Baldwin crawled into the clearing with a platter of sliders. "Who's ready for more? Ah, Sophia. You've joined us. Excellent."

He offered her a burger. She felt disloyal eating Chef Baldwin's tapas, but she was starving.

"Thank you. I'll try one." It was stacked high with pickled cucumbers and tomatoes, and delicious with the beer.

Michael sat down next to her and immediately pressed his thigh against her leg.

"So tell us the truth, lovely garden fairy. Are you regretting your choice of partner? Everyone wants to know." Michael leaned close enough for Sophia to smell his cologne. There was something incongruous about cologne in the woods of

Vermont. It was a city smell, a city behavior. She leaned back in her chair.

"Not at all. Elliott is an extremely talented chef."

"And also an extreme pain-in-the-ass. Don't tell me you haven't noticed."

"Everyone has their own way of doing things. It will take some time for us to figure out to work together."

"So very diplomatic." Michael looked unconvinced.

Sophia attempted to change the subject. "Why don't you and Helene and Lin Lin tell us about your restaurants? I would love to hear about that."

The professional chefs dived right into that topic. Sophia was relieved, although Michael was touching her quite a bit as he spoke. Squeezing her knee. Brushing against her arm. And she hadn't failed to notice him staring at her breasts. Dear Lord. It had been a while since she'd flirted with anyone, but this was awkward.

She leaned farther back in her chair, until the rustling branches of the willow draped along her shoulders. Her arms dangled behind her, out of Michael's reach.

And then she felt the brush of fingers on her hand. But not from Michael.

And a gentle squeeze.

And then broad fingers linked with hers, tightening in her grasp.

"Mind if I join you?" That delicious Scottish burr raised up all the hairs on the back of her neck.

Elliott placed a seat behind the group, so that he was still somewhat sheltered by the weeping branches.

Helene laughed. "You Scots are so sneaky, *n'est-ce pas*? How long have you been hiding there, Elliott?"

"Long enough to see Sophia eating a burger. Was it good, Sprite? Should I try one?"

His eyes sparkled. And she realized that not all flirting was clumsy and suggestive.

She held the burger for Elliott to try, and he leaned

forward and took a bite. His eyes watched hers, unblinking, as he slowly chewed the tapas. When he finished, he gave her a half-smile. Teasing.

"Hmm. Not half bad. I might have to stop giving Baldwin so much shit."

Michael didn't look pleased to have Elliott join them. "I won't hold my breath."

Helene laughed. "Sophia, I was wondering about the salad you made today. It looked so beautiful with all the bright greens. Tell me about it."

"I call that one 'hide-the-peas.' My daughters are college-age now, but when they were little, they hated to eat their green vegetables. I tried every possible way to entice them. One day we started a game. I hid all sorts of vegetables in the salad, and the girls got points when they 'discovered' the different greens and ate them. Asparagus, peas, zucchini. It worked like a charm."

"That was your family recipe?" Elliott asked, looking thoughtful.

"Yes. More like the act of a desperate mother."

"You don't look old enough to have college-age kids, S-Sophia." Tammy shot her a shy smile.

"Oh, but I am. I can count my white hairs to prove it."

Michael reached out and wrapped a piece of her hair around his fist. "Your hair is lovely. And the bits of silver are part of the appeal."

Elliott tensed and didn't relax until Chef Baldwin released the strand of hair. Her partner leaned closer, so close the heat of his body warmed her back. He found her hand again and snagged it, tethering her to him in the safety of the shadows. Elliott hid his need for her, but was adamant about his possession. He tugged her away from Baldwin, angling her body towards his own.

Elliott was confusing the hell out of her.

Someone shouted for Michael, and he reluctantly stood

to leave. He glanced at Sophia, who was now semi-hidden in a snarl of branches with Elliott practically draped around her. Chef Baldwin shook his head and left.

Elliott finally relaxed. He finished off Sophia's sliders and happily accepted a beer from Nathan. The group continued to chat until the fireflies darted under the canopy.

"Come with me," Elliott whispered in Sophia's ear.

She turned her head slightly and could barely make out the outline of his face.

"What?"

"Come with me. We need to talk." Elliott squeezed her hand again, this time with less desperation. "Come with me, Sophia."

She nodded, not quite sure if he could see the gesture in the darkness.

Was this how he had seduced his wives? The brush of hand? A whisper in the shadows? Because it was working like a charm with her.

The good little widow slipped away with Elliott into the night.

🖉 🖉 🖉

Elliott took her to a pond on the outskirts of the campus. Sophia wondered if he'd spent the afternoon exploring Vermont, searching for something along dirt trails and rocky outcrops. The night was black and quiet, the sort of quiet that shocked city folk and comforted those who lived here. He continued over a footbridge and stopped at the apex. Dots of light from the lampposts rippled on the surface of the water. Frogs croaked from somewhere inside the tall grass.

"Good thing Helene isn't here. She'd gather up those frogs and serve *cuisses de grenouille* for the next challenge." Elliott skipped a stone on the pond, and several frogs voiced their displeasure.

"Hmm. I'm not sure Vermont frogs are plump enough for that. I'll leave that dish in Helene's capable hands."

Elliott turned to her and smiled. "I've made *cuisses de grenouille* many times. It's expected when you study French cuisine."

"Do you like it?" Sophia was still not sure why she was here. Or what Elliott hoped to accomplish.

"Yes, quite a lot actually. I used to include specialties from different European regions on my menu. That was before I decided to focus solely on traditional Scottish fare." He leaned against the railing on the bridge. "I liked your story about hiding the peas. It's obvious your culinary inspiration is your family."

"Of course. I cook for them."

Elliott nodded, his forehead creased. "I have never had a partner, Sophia. I cook alone. I work alone. I create alone. This whole thing is way out of my comfort zone."

"What about your wives?"

He blanched. "Not partners. Maybe…assistants. They helped with the prep work, cleaning, that sort of thing. Everything on my menu is my own creation. Mine alone."

"Your wives…were *sous-chefs*. Dear Lord, Elliott. Didn't it ever occur to you—?"

"No," he answered irritably. "Let's get back to the matter at hand. *A Taste of Heaven.* As much as it pains me to admit I need some help, I need some help. With Jenny the Blogger on the judging panel, I need some connection to the American palate." He tapped his fingers on the wooden rail. "I need your help."

"You have it. You always have." She took a step closer to him.

"I don't like to lose. I'm…tired of it. I'm tired."

And that, thought Sophia, must be the understatement of the year. After losing three restaurants and three marriages and then watching his contemporaries rise to the top as he struggled for respect within the culinary world.

He must be bone-tired. And she knew the feeling.

Elliott blew out a long breath. "God must have been looking out for me, since I got paired with you instead of the others. You're smart and thoughtful. It could be a lot worse."

Sophia laughed softly. "I'm bowled over by that effusive praise."

Elliott stroked his beard. "You'll get my praise when you knock my socks off. That hasn't happened yet."

"So what do you need, Chef Adamson?"

"I need to know what makes you tick. Who you are. What will be your strongest contribution to our combined effort? Tell me, Sophia. Who are you?"

She wanted to burst out laughing. Who was she? What a ridiculous question.

"I don't have any idea how to answer that. What are you really asking me?"

Elliott leaned down to her eye level. The heavy fragrance of wild *Rosa* and honeysuckle mixed with the scent of Elliott. So close to her. Too close. She had to watch herself around this man. And not get dragged into his drama. She had to remember that he left women behind like shriveled-up carcasses in the road.

Sous-chef indeed.

"If you had to make your perfect meal, what would it be? For you and your family. The perfect evening. Tell me. This is how we're going to win. I need to get into your head, figure out how to weave the two of us together."

"Weave us together like a blanket?" She cocked her head, amused by the intensity in his gaze.

"Yes. Like a blanket. A gourmet blanket that appeals to Tarquin's quirky taste, Jonathan's need for balance, Jenny's love of decoration. Tell me about your perfect evening."

She smiled. "That's an easy question. Any night with my daughters, especially in the summer. We eat outside next to the garden. There are mason jars strung up in the tree branches, filled with beeswax candles. We stay out until it's pitch black and starry. The girls always help with dinner. It…" She felt herself tearing up. "They are so sweet. Cady, my youngest, is the adventurous one. And artistic. Her food is very visual and bright. Em is more straight-forward. She likes to follow a recipe. To a T. More like her father."

Elliott took Sophia's face in his hands, and she forgot to breathe.

"Close your eyes, Sophia. Look at the table in your mind. What does it look like? What's on the menu? Taste it. Tell me."

She closed her eyes. Enveloped by all that was Elliott. She tried to concentrate and ignore those rough fingers on her cheek.

"Shrimp wrapped in Thai basil and prosciutto, crisped on the grill, drizzled with olive oil and fresh lime juice. It's Emilia's favorite."

"Mmm. Keep going. Don't stop."

His lips were almost touching her forehead. His breath on her skin.

"Grilled filet mignon with my peppercorn sauce. White, red, pink peppercorns. The girls get them for me when they travel. That's our special dinner. Our decadent meal."

"More." His lips grazed her ear.

Sophia's eyes were still tightly shut, but she had to suppress a shudder.

"Vegetable salad on baby greens from my garden. Yellow peppers, green zucchini, purple eggplant, lightly grilled. With a sherry vinaigrette and fresh herbs. All the colors of the rainbow."

"Lovely. Keep going."

She could no longer hear the buzz of crickets or throaty calls of the frogs. Just Elliott's breathing. Steady. Intense.

"Wine, lots of wine," she said huskily.

She felt his chuckle against her cheek.

"Well, this is my fantasy, right? It must have wine."

"Of course it does. Keep going."

"Home-made gelato. Lemon. With lemon zest and lemon

basil and lemon verbena. And crunchy toasted macadamia nuts on top. Cady just got back from service camp in Hawaii. I have a lot of macadamia nuts in my pantry right now."

He laughed. A full-blown laugh against the side of her face.

"And my table is set with things that remind me of people I love and places I've visited. Places I care about. My Depression Era goblets are from the antique fair I attend every year with Emilia. The pottery plates Cady made in art class. David bought me the miniature flower vases at a local glass-blowing shop. My sister wove our place mats."

Sophia opened her eyes. Elliott was staring at her intently.

"What? Too hodge-podge and mismatched?"

"No. It sounds perfectly wonderful." Those intense indigo eyes captured her gaze and refused to let go.

Instantly she felt stripped, naked. Was he judging her? Her pathetic best night. Simple and lacking in excitement? Did he see the comfort in that? Why it touched her so much?

Sophia cleared her throat. "So did you figure out what you needed to know?"

"Yes. Your flavors are clean, seasonal, bright. You like lemon."

They both laughed.

"You cook to please the ones you love. You surround yourself with good memories." He paused. "Does it work? The memories? Does it make you happy?"

She sighed. "The jury's still out on that one. It used to. It's been more difficult recently. I'll let you know when I figure it out."

He nodded and kissed her cheek. A brush of his beard, the warmth of his mouth, over and gone before she had a chance to savor it.

"Tomorrow is a new day. And Sophia..."

"Yes, Elliott?"

"Tomorrow we *win*."

Chapter Thirteen

Elliott was in high spirits the next morning. He actually sat next to Sophia on the van ride to their undisclosed location. He was quiet, but alert and absorbed enough to ignore the usual taunts from Baldwin and the others. She took this as a good sign. When she reached over to squeeze his hand, he grabbed it and refused to relinquish it until they arrived at their destination. As they exited the van, he whispered in her ear, *"Winning Day."*

And now Mr. Smith had herded them like a bunch of cattle inside a fence at Rigley's Creamery. She had an uneasy feeling about today's challenge. The interns were whispering and scurrying about.

"Welcome to Rigley's Creamery, home of Vermont's most delectable cheese!" Mr. Smith boomed his introduction in front of the factory.

The contestants looked wary. Mr. Smith had a suspicious gleam in his eye.

"Today we will be focusing on cheese, one of the premiere

products of Vermont. And what a selection we have at Rigley's...chevre, blue, cheddar. Anything your heart desires."

"How about something Scottish, like Arran cheddar. That's what I desire," Elliott whispered.

"A snob to the bitter end. I think you'll be impressed with this cheese, Chef Adamson. It's excellent. Quit yer complaining," Sophia whispered back.

Elliott chuckled.

"All of our contestants will be highlighting this wonderful ingredient for their meal. However, there is one little hitch." Mr. Smith smiled and pointed to the main barn. "What is that I hear? The pitter-patter of little feet?"

The barn doors flew open and dozens of children raced into the courtyard. All of the contestants groaned in unison. Sophia smiled. If there was one thing she knew, and she knew well, it was how to feed children. Picky children. Messy, cranky, unpredictable children.

The kids were yelling and stampeding around. It took a few minutes for the producers to settle them down.

"As you can see, your customers today are eight years old, third graders from Norwich Elementary School. We're going to be preparing a delicious lunch for these youngsters using the award-winning cheese. The judging panel will be looking at how well you have incorporated the local products into your meal, in addition to how appropriate your dish is for this youthful audience. You have fifteen minutes to discuss your menus with your partners, and then time will start for this challenge. You'll be cooking in the Rigley kitchens, which are fully stocked with organic proteins and produce. Lunch will be served outside in three hours."

Sophia piped up. "What will the children be doing for the next three hours?"

"Helping on the farm. Milking the cows, feeding the chickens and gathering eggs. They'll be good and hungry by lunch time."

She turned to Elliott, ready for a sarcastic comment

or cutting remark. Instead she found him white-faced and panicked.

"Elliott, what's wrong?"

"I…I can't do this."

"You can't do what?"

"This. Making food for youngsters." He squeezed her hand so hard Sophia was worried he'd crushed her fingers.

"Of course you can. We can do this together."

He shook his head. "No, you don't understand. I don't like kids. I don't offer a children's menu at my restaurants. I don't like 'watering down' my dishes or serving fish sticks for the wee ones. I just don't do it."

"Elliott—"

"This is going to be a disaster. All of my best recipes with cheese include whisky!"

"Elliott." She gripped his arm. "Snap out of it."

He looked broken already, and the challenge hadn't started yet.

"What happened to our new winning attitude? It's gone already?"

"I never expected this. I thought I would be cooking for *adults*."

In addition to being stubborn and single-minded, Elliott Adamson was clearly lacking in flexibility, which was a prerequisite for a contest like this. He just needed a nudge in the right direction.

"Well, guess what? It's your lucky day. You have an ace in the hole."

He rubbed his hands over his face in a defeated gesture. "What's that?"

"Me. You have me."

He said nothing.

"I have kids."

He perked up somewhat at that comment.

"Two kids. Two picky kids. And I spent years of my life figuring out how to cook for them and entice them to eat."

Elliott's expression turned attentive. "Keep talking."

"First of all, tell me your favorite Scottish cheese recipes. Let's figure out how we can adapt them. We can do this."

He nodded slowly and the color began to return to his face. "Cauliflower, cheese, and whisky soup."

"That sounds delicious."

"It is. But I don't think these wee ones are ready for Scotch whisky."

She smiled. "We omit the whisky."

"But—"

"No, we'll add the kick in another way. That soup sounds like something kids would love. My girls adored cheese soup. And I made it with Vermont cheddar."

His jaw clenched. Sophia waited for him to come to terms with this new development.

He released a haggard breath. "Wh-What else did your girls like to eat?"

"Cheddar soup, grilled cheese sandwiches cut up into little triangles. Crunchy cheese sticks. It's got different textures, it's fun to eat. Cady and Em loved it. These kids will love it, too."

"Grilled cheese? Is that really going to win a competition like this?"

"It could if the kids like it. The producer said that was an integral part of this contest. We just need to elevate the sandwich, but still make it appealing to the children."

Elliott frowned. "Do you think they'd like grilled ham-and-cheese?"

"Yes! That's a great idea. My girls loved that combination. And how about we add some of the orange marmalade I made for the first challenge? That might be a nice sweet condiment."

Elliott scribbled in his notebook. "Okay." He nodded. "I have to bow to your experience, as much as that pains me." He shot her a look. "And believe me, it pains me."

"I didn't go to culinary school, and I'm not an expert on

Scottish cuisine. But I fed my daughters for two decades. I know kids. We can do this. Together." She laid her hand on his forearm.

Elliott glanced down at her hand. His face was blank, emotionless. He was struggling with this shift in power. With this loss of control.

"All right. *Don't* let me down."

Please, God, let this work.

They began to discuss their menu. She watched Chef Adamson weigh her suggestions. Dissect her ideas. His eyes darted from her face back to his notebook. He scribbled, and scratched, and then underlined his thoughts. For the first time, she got a sense of what it was truly like to collaborate with this man. None of his ideas were spur-of-moment or quickly considered. He mulled over the ideas, flipped them, let them percolate, added and subtracted. It was an exhausting process. But she began to see the way his brain worked. How he pulled from years of experience, different cultures, different techniques, and by the time he was done, he had a menu that was thoughtful and clear. And as they finished their discussion, it was obvious that she had gained a grudging respect from her partner. Only because she was an experienced mother. But she had to start somewhere. Earning his trust.

She was starting with a grilled cheese sandwich.

They were given the go-ahead to begin cooking. All of the chefs scrambled about collecting ingredients and commencing their prep work. Elliott chopped vegetables for the stock… cauliflower, carrots, parsnips, artichokes. Sophia grated the sharp cheddar cheese and scooped it into a wooden bowl.

"Dammit, Harold. You need to do something about her. She's in way over her head."

Sophia glanced over her shoulder to find Jonathan Rutgers in a hushed and heated argument with their producer Harold Smith.

"There's nothing I can do about it now, Jonathan. We've

already taped half the show. She's staying."

"She's obnoxious and completely lacking in any sort of culinary knowledge."

"It's good to have someone more relatable and accessible on the judging panel. You and Tarquin are culinary big-wigs. Our audience at home can relate to Jenny." Mr. Smith wiped his forehead with his favorite linen hankie. "It will be okay. You'll see."

"She's been inappropriate with me. I'm married. She's been inappropriate with Tarquin. He's *gay*, for God's sake. The woman is a complete ding-bat."

"Look. There are only a few more days of taping. You can do this. Think about how great the exposure will be for you when you release your cookbook. Just try to ignore the blogger."

Chef Rutgers shook his head. "Fine. But keep her away from me. Tarquin doesn't seem to mind so much. He thinks the whole situation is amusing." Jonathan frowned. "I, however, do not." He stormed off. Mr. Smith sighed and hustled over to the camera crew.

"Ignore them, Sophia." Elliott continued to chop vegetables for his soup.

"Did you hear that? I wondered what Tarquin and Jonathan thought about Jenny," Sophia whispered back.

"Try to ignore the melodrama. There's always something going on in the kitchen. Fighting, loving, jealousy, hostility. You need to block that all out and just focus on the food. That's all that matters. The food."

"That's easier said than done in a competition like this. There's drama on-set, off-set, even at our field locations. I saw Harold fighting with a farmer yesterday at Loden Farm. Tempers are high."

"It's human nature, and the culinary industry thrives on the competitive aspect. The farmer probably felt marginalized by the crew and producers. The amateurs are resentful of the professional chefs." He stopped and studied her. "The classically-trained chefs pooh-pooh the new trends with molecular gastronomy. And of course the American palates see haggis and gag." He raised an eyebrow at Sophia. "We ignore the fighting, the feuding opinions, the bickering and conflict. We cook. And we cook well."

Sophia laughed. "Good advice, Chef Adamson. We cook." She held up a hunk of cheese. "We cook cheese."

Elliott released a strained chuckle and continued mincing.

Mr. Smith interrupted their work to encourage the chefs. "How's it going, contestants? Is everyone ready to feed your *very short* customers today?"

"Ugh. That was a piss-poor joke." Elliott rolled his eyes.

Short Chubby Guy yelled, "It's all about the cheese!"

Mr. Smith waved the damned flag over his head. "Get cooking! We're ready for *A Taste of Heaven*!"

Elliott leaned close to Sophia and captured her gaze with his indigo eyes. Blazing so fiercely they took her breath away. "We're winning today, goddammit. Do you hear me? *Winning*."

Sophia nodded. "I heard you."

The flag slashed through the air.

✐ ✐ ✐

This might be the first time in history that judges table disintegrated into a food fight. Sophia had a fleeting recollection of the movie *Animal House*. The children smelled horrible, probably covered with compost and muck. They were sweaty and antsy and obviously starving. She wasn't sure what the producers had planned for the next part of the show, but she hoped lunch would be served within the next thirty seconds, or all hell was about to break loose at Rigley's Creamery.

Mr. Smith swallowed nervously as he surveyed the banquet table. Out came the linen handkerchief as he wiped his forehead. He cleared his throat, but the children completely ignored him.

A loud, screeching whistle brought everyone to a standstill.

Mr. Smith turned to the chefs, eyes wide with surprise.

"It looked like you could use a spot of help with the kidlets. Noisy bunch, aren't they?" Elliott's face showed no emotion.

Sophia had to bite her lip to keep from laughing.

"Um, thank you, Chef Adamson." Mr. Smith faced the children. "Who's ready for lunch?"

The answering war cry was deafening. A river of sweat ran down the side of the producer's face.

Mr. Smith turned to the contestants in desperation. "Who's up first?"

One after another, the pairs brought plates to the table. Lunch never broke down into an all-out food fight, but Sophia did spy some vegetables on the ground. She heard compliments, insults, and plenty of laughter. She envied the children those simple moments. Eating with friends. Giggling at jokes. When your day's biggest obstacle was whether or not you could swallow a spear of asparagus.

Finally it was their turn to present. Elliott regarded the children with a mix of mistrust and hostility. Sophia would have to do the bulk of the presentation today.

"Elliott and Sophia, what are you serving for our hungry clients this afternoon?" Mr. Smith was most likely dreaming about his first scotch at cocktail hour.

Sophia stepped forward, and Elliott let her. She glanced at him and he gestured for her to get on with it. Clearly he had no issue with her speaking up.

"We have a delicious treat for the kids today. One of my daughters' favorite lunches…soup and grilled cheese sandwiches. We also made crunchy cheese sticks."

The children cheered. She noticed some of the boys having sword fights with the cheese sticks. Whatever made them happy. She had assembled fruit "flowers" on the plates as a garnish, and they loved those. She huffed out a sigh of relief.

Tarquin ushered the chefs to the side of the table. "And how about a more detailed description for the adult judges?"

Relieved to leave the children's table, Elliott turned his back on them and addressed the judges. "The soup is based on a traditional Scottish cauliflower cheese soup. I made a rich stock with ten assorted vegetables from the Rigley organic garden. We used their extra sharp cheddar and the double cream to thicken the soup. The sandwiches include soft muenster, slices of smoked ham, and a dollop of the Scottish marmalade for sweetness."

Jenny smiled. "How did you make those crispy cheese sticks? The kids seem to really love them."

Sophia answered. "We incorporated Parmesan and fresh dill in the dough."

"And the fruit flowers? I have a sneaking suspicion that was not the work of our Scottish chef."

Elliott grumbled under his breath.

Sophia raised a brow. "I made the flowers. My girls loved it when I made vignettes with fruits and vegetables on their plates."

"Well," Jenny answered, "these kids love them, too. Very sweet."

"Who was in charge of this menu, Chef Adamson?" Jonathan Rutgers began his interrogation.

Elliott hesitated. He glanced at Sophia, and she was surprised to see gratitude mixed with some underlying discomfiture. He answered stiffly. "My partner and I...collaborated on this meal. I adapted an old favorite to be... child-friendly. The original soup recipe includes whisky. We decided to leave that out today."

The judges laughed. "That was an intelligent decision," Tarquin said.

"You covered all your bases with this challenge. You

included a nice assortment of the Vermont cheeses, you made a well-balanced and healthy meal in terms of textures and sides. And most importantly, the kids love it." Jenny was clearly impressed.

"Why don't we ask the kids what they thought?" Tarquin said. He approached the table and began to interview the children.

"This was my favorite! I love this soup."

"The bread sticks are good. I want my mom to make this for me."

"I like the grilled cheese, but I took off the ham. I don't like ham."

Elliott rolled his eyes, but Sophia was charmed. And relieved. This reminded her of lunch times from more than a decade ago, when David was still alive and the girls were little. Emilia and Cady and their merry band of friends would run into the house, dirty and hot and ready to eat. She smiled at the children as she reminisced.

A little girl waved to Sophia and she waved back.

"Thanks, Chef Brown. I love this lunch."

"You're very welcome."

All of the kids waved and laughed, and she giggled with them. Elliott looked utterly perplexed. She had to lift his arm to wave it, which made the kids laugh even harder.

"Well, well, well, someone is quite charming on camera. Very well done, Sophia." Mr. Smith whispered close to her ear, and he looked exceedingly pleased.

The final contestants delivered their platters, and soon it was time for the finalists to be announced. Sophia noticed that the majority of the chefs made sophisticated meals and ignored their audience. She wondered if the adult judges would still give them good marks for preparing high-quality food, or if they would be critical of that point.

Tarquin smiled for the camera. "Today's challenge seemed to throw our chefs off their game. I'm surprised. Cheese is an easy ingredient. That was a give-away."

Jenny shook her head. "But cooking for kids was the tough part. And I know. I have three gorgeous pumpkins at home—Grace, Joseph, and Mary Kate. And each one of them wants to eat a different meal. Kids are a *big* challenge in the kitchen."

Jonathan Rutgers's face was expressionless, but Sophia could see the tick jumping on his cheek.

"Honestly, three of our remaining pairs were a huge disappointment today. But the one pair that really missed the mark was Lin Lin and Tammy. That meal was way too sophisticated for third graders. Most of them refused to eat it. I'm sorry to say that you two are the losing pair for this challenge," Jenny said.

Lin Lin shot an angry look at the remaining chefs and shuffled off the set with her partner.

"We really only had two pairs that fulfilled the requirements today. Brian and Herman. And Elliott and Sophia. Why don't you four step forward?" Mr. Smith gestured for the finalists to join him.

Elliott blew out a long, slow hiss. His face was pale and tense. He pressed a hand against Sophia's lower back and escorted her to the judging table.

They were so close. *So close!*

"Chefs Brian and Herman made pizza, a perfect way to please a younger customer, in addition to incorporating the fresh Rigley Creamery mozzarella. And Chefs Elliott and Sophia prepared a rich soup and golden fried cheese sandwiches. With some whimsical fruit garnishes. Well-played." Jonathan nodded in their direction.

"The other contestants were a bit too focused on making complicated dishes that showed off their cooking techniques." Jenny frowned. "Kids don't care about that. They just want food that's tasty and doesn't scare the pants off them."

Mr. Smith cleared his throat. "Well, judges, who is the winner today? It's Battle Pizza Versus Grilled Cheese."

Jenny clapped her hands. "The kids' decision was

unanimous, and the judges agreed. Sophia and Elliott won this round."

Finally!

Sophia laughed out loud. Elliott sagged with relief. He crushed her in his arms, and she could feel his body trembling. When he pulled away to face the judges, she was surprised to see tension lines still creasing his forehead.

"You're lucky you didn't serve haggis to the kids. We would have had a rebellion on our hands." Jenny shot Elliott a venomous smile.

"God forbid. Good thing Chef Brown was here to keep me reined in."

Elliott's sarcastic response lacked emotion, but Sophia could tell his antagonism for the blogger was about to explode.

She touched his arm lightly, trying to reassure him. Trying to breach his wall and figure out what was wrong.

He ignored her.

"Yes," Mr. Smith agreed, "you are a lucky man, Chef Adamson. I think Sophia was the crowd favorite today."

That was clearly not what Elliott wanted to hear. He nodded tersely and refused to make eye contact with her. She wanted to throttle him. They won. *They won!* And he was still not satisfied.

"Well, look at her. She's adorable and plays in the garden. Why wouldn't she be the crowd favorite?" Elliott glanced at Sophia, and when he saw her barely suppressed anger, he sighed. "Congratulations, Sophia. Well done." He leaned over and kissed her on the mouth.

On the mouth!

The kiss was quick, and filled with gratitude, and also brimming with tension.

Damn that man.

Short Chubby Guy yelled, "Grumpy Scottish Bastard wins!"

The other contestants laughed, but Mr. Smith did not look amused. That would have to be censored out of the final cut.

Finally the crew wrapped up filming. Elliott walked away, without saying a word to his partner.

Not a word.

Damn that man!

"Mrs. Brown, may I bend your ear?" Mr. Smith asked. "Congratulations on your win today. You really captured the hearts of those children."

Sophia shrugged. "I have two daughters and lots of experience cooking for kids."

Mr. Smith nodded. "I could tell. But it's more than that, Sophia. You have a presence in front of the camera—gracious and sweet. Approachable. Your love for gardening and using fresh local products comes through with all of your dishes. And you take the recipes and make them accessible for everyone. That's not an easy thing to do."

Sophia struggled to hide her blush. "Well, I taught my daughters to cook. I guess that requires patience. I never really thought about it."

"*I'm* thinking about it," the producer answered. "I'm thinking you may have a future in television. I can see you as host of a children's cooking show. Or a gardening-cooking show. Anything, really. You have that special something that is unpredictable in this industry. You're beautiful in front of the camera, but also humble and genuine. The Creativity Channel would *love* to have you on board."

Sophia was speechless. "I don't know what to say."

"Think about it. After this contest airs, you'll be a household name. You can use that exposure in any direction you choose. I would be thrilled to have you on our spring schedule."

"I'll…I'll…think about it. Thank you for the vote of confidence."

"I know a future star when I see one." Mr. Smith winked at her and ambled away.

A future star? How ludicrous. Wasn't it? Could it possibly be real? A fresh new start that wasn't part of "David and

Sophia?" That was just Sophia. Was she brave enough to even consider it?

Regardless of her future in television, regardless of Elliott's sour disposition, Sophia was filled with pride. She'd won that contest today. It was her experience with children that made the difference. It was her creative vision on the plate. She had guided Elliott, and not the other way around. She smiled to herself, filled with a growing sense of awe about her own capabilities. Filled with a growing excitement, if not uncertainty, about the future.

She would ponder Mr. Smith's offer later. For now she needed to focus on one thing. Reaching the finals of *A Taste of Heaven*. And unless she figured out how to break down Elliott's wall of anger, she highly doubted they had a chance at winning.

Damn that man.

 Chapter
Fourteen

Sophia pounded on Elliott's dormitory door. "Elliott! I know you're in there. Let me in."

"Go away, Sprite." His words sounded slightly slurred.

"No. I'm not going away. I'm not going anywhere until you talk to me."

"Go. *Away*."

She smacked the flat of her hand against the door.

He ignored her.

She began a regular pounding rhythm. He lasted for two minutes, and then he flung open the door.

"What the hell are you doing? Leave me *alone*. Alone. Alone. What part of—?"

She interrupted and pushed him aside. "I'm coming in now. We're going to talk, whether you like it or not."

"Not. I like it *not*." He sloshed his highball glass in front of her face. "Care to join me? Since you're here. Bugging the hell out of me." His request was dripping with sarcasm.

"No, thank you. I don't like whisky. I prefer wine."

"How very civilized of you. Miss Priss. Miss Prissy Children-Hugging Garden Fairy Priss."

She plopped down on his bed. "Isn't it nice to finally have the room all to yourself?"

He sat on the bed across from her. "Aye. A real luxurious treat since Mr. Burnside-from-Oklahoma was eliminated yesterday. Too bad he missed today's cheese challenge."

Sophia cocked her head. "Care to discuss it?"

"No."

"I think you need to. You're pissed, Elliott. And I don't get it. You told me you had to win. This is what you wanted. You made me promise. I did everything you asked. We *won*."

"*No! We* did not win. *We* did not win. *You* won. *You* won. I'm—"

"You egotistical bastard."

"Yes. I am. Do you have any idea how utterly humiliating it is that a little housewife from the suburbs made grilled-*fucking*-cheese-sandwiches for a bunch of snotty-nosed kids, and we won! What kind of ludicrous contest is this?"

"Oh my God. You are unbelievable."

"Yes, I am. Unbelievable. But unfortunately, those kids wouldn't know *unbelievable* if it bit them on their wee little bums. And Jenny the Blogger wouldn't know *unbelievable* if it slipped through her collagen-enhanced lips. And—"

"That's enough."

"Really? I thought you wanted to talk." He sneered the last word and finished off his whisky. "Uh-oh. My glass is empty." He walked over to the dresser and opened a bottle of Scotch.

"Take it easy with that, Elliott. You're going to be hung over tomorrow. That's not a good idea."

"What the hell difference will it make? I'm just a line cook. Line cooks get pissed all the time."

Sophia sighed and slumped down on his bed. This was going to be more difficult than she'd thought. "Elliott, you're not a line cook. You're captain of the team, remember? I need your guidance and help if we're going to win this whole thing. We're on the way."

"Aye. The way to nowhere." He glanced at her. "You're looking lovely, lass. All pink-cheeked and tousled. You know what everyone will say when you leave my room."

"What? That I'm still alive? Maybe they'll make me a *I Survived Elliott Adamson* T-shirt."

He chuckled. "Maybe they will." He swallowed another sip of Scotch. "So you don't like whisky, huh?"

She narrowed her eyes. Why was he changing the subject? "Not my favorite drink."

"Why not?"

"I think it tastes like gasoline."

Elliott joined her on the bed. He lifted her chin with his finger. "Time for you to get an education about whisky. It doesn't taste like petrol. It tastes like fire." He handed her the glass. "This is thirty-year aged Lagavulin, made in Islay, Scotland. It tastes like peat. Like smoke. Rich and thick. Put a small bit on your tongue and let it seep into your soul. Don't tell me it tastes like *gasoline*."

Sophia rolled her eyes and sipped. "Okay, now can we talk."

"Another sip."

"Elliott!"

"Do it. Savor it."

She took another sip, and let the fire burn down her throat. If Elliott had a taste, she bet it would be this. Hot and smoky and strong.

"Well? Better?" Elliott's eyes looked drowsy. Sexy.

She swallowed another sip. "The color is so beautiful. Like amber."

"Hmm. Yes." He licked his lips.

"So, about today…"

"No more talking about today. No more talking at all." Elliott lifted the glass from her hands and set it on the dinged-up table next to the bed.

He brushed her lips with his fingers. Rough callused skin against her lips, still wet with whisky.

Sophia wished that gesture didn't make her breath catch.

She shook her head. "I sure hope you're not planning to seduce me. Is that the plan? Get Sophia drunk and have your wicked way with her?" Her voice was ragged. She could hear her heartbeat.

"That sounds like a plan."

"That sounds like a horrible plan. We have to work together."

"I worked with my wives."

"Your sous-chefs, you mean. I remember. They weren't allowed to work your side. I'm not interested in being cast aside after I clean the pots, Chef Adamson."

He frowned. "I would never do that to you. You're…different. Not like the others, Sophia. Not like the others."

She stood. "I'd better go. Please go to bed. I need you fresh and well-rested for the next challenge. We don't know what tomorrow will bring." She walked to the door.

He followed her.

Sophia barely turned her head. "Good night, Elliott," she whispered. Trying to ignore the scent of whisky and peat and Elliott, all mixed together like some intoxicating liquid, ready to slosh right onto her lips.

His hand pressed against the door, holding it shut. "Sophia." His voice was rough.

She closed her eyes. Elliott's heat and hardness pressed against her back. She swallowed once. Twice. Wishing for another sip of Lagavulin.

For a sip of him.

"Sophia." His voice was barely a whisper. He grasped her waist, bunching up her faded T-shirt.

"Elliott." She shivered. "We shouldn't…"

"I know. But give me this. I promise I won't fail. Not with this." His beard brushed against her face, and he nipped her earlobe. "Let's be honest. You won that contest today, not I. You succeeded where I failed. You led us to victory while I fumbled." He unsnapped her jeans and slid his fingers into her panties. "But this…I promise you. *This* is something I'm good at."

Sophia twisted her neck to look at Elliott's face. It was filled with so much raw emotion, it took her breath away. *You haven't failed, Elliott. You haven't failed me.*

"I need this. Let me have you. Just…like this." Elliott dragged his fingers over her pubic hair, touching softly.

Sophia moaned and nodded. She couldn't help it. It had been so long, and his explorations felt delicious. Maybe she could indulge.

Maybe for just a moment.

She swayed, and Elliott held her up with one arm. The other arm was moving against her. Searching for things she couldn't resist.

"Open your legs. Wider. Do this for me, Sophia."

And she did.

She let Elliott Adamson touch her and stroke her and find the sweet spot that pushed her right over the edge. Pushed up against the dorm room door. With his heavy breathing in her ear and desperation etched all over his face.

And after she cried out and shuddered in his arms, he held her and kissed her cheek, grazing that thick beard over her tears.

"Thank you, Sophia. Go back to your room and sleep. I promise tomorrow I'll be the man you need."

It was late. The halls were empty.

She staggered back to her room.

Chapter Fifteen

Sophia lay in her rickety bed and stared at the ceiling. She stared at the cracks in the plaster that crisscrossed the walls. In all of her forty-seven years, she had never done anything as salacious as last night's interlude.

Not in high school, when she groped the soccer player in his basement. Not in college, when she got drunk at a party and slept with her girlfriend's cousin. Certainly not after she met David. They'd had an active sex life, but it was very conventional. Safe. Expected.

Last night was both unexpected and secretly thrilling.

They'd skipped first base. They'd skipped second base. They'd skipped half of third. Only she got her third, not Elliott.

She covered her face with her hands as a blush ripped over her cheeks.

Dear Lord! How am I ever going to look at him today?

Only half of third, but damn. That was a good half. Fast and furious. She ought to be embarrassed by how quickly he'd got her off. But instead she was just curious about the bases they'd skipped. She wanted his hands on her breasts. She wanted his mouth on her lips. But she needed to focus on today's challenge. Could there be a bigger distraction than the replayed memory of Elliott Adamson's rough fingers sliding into her panties?

Probably not.

She shouldn't have worried. When she finally ran into Elliott later in the morning—at the Jefferson Turkey Farm—he acted like nothing had happened. Not a stutter, not a blush. Not a suggestive eyebrow raise. Absolutely nothing. Sophia wasn't sure if she should be relieved or disappointed.

But she soon realized that Elliott was keyed up in a major way. Interns and camera crew congratulated him on the win from yesterday, and he barely nodded an acknowledgement. Sophia could tell he was embarrassed about the whole event. Even though it finally got them a win.

She sighed and pushed her hair back into a ponytail. She wasn't sure what the producers had in mind at the turkey farm, but she wasn't interested in getting salmonella juice on her hair.

When they had the eight remaining chefs put on full-length overalls, she started to get really worried.

"Welcome back to *A Taste of Heaven*!" Mr. Smith smiled at them and pretended to ignore the camera. "I'm sure you're all wondering why we're here at the Jefferson Turkey Farm. And why you're dressed like that." He chuckled. "We're down to the four final pairs—Sophia and Elliott, Michael and Kevin, Brian and Herman, and finally Helene and Nathan. Some of you are very lucky to be here, after yesterday's surprisingly difficult challenge. Who knew a bunch of kids would throw everyone off their game?"

As Harold continued to talk, one of the farmers brought out a selection of axes and machetes. Sophia felt light-headed.

"Oh my God," she whispered to Elliott.

"This ought to separate the men from the boys. No fruit flower today, Sophia." He glanced at her. "Think you can handle this? You look pale."

"I don't know. I've watched my girlfriend do it, but... I don't know. I'm sorry."

"Don't be sorry, Sprite. I've got this one covered."

She was more than slightly concerned when she looked at her partner. He had a gleam in his eye.

Mr. Smith lifted an axe. "Today's game is a bit messier. And perhaps a bit intimidating."

Sophia heard Herman make a retching sound. She didn't think it was faked for the camera.

Mr. Smith continued. "Part of the whole farm-to-table concept is following the path of raising animals in a humane and thoughtful way to butchering them and then preparing them for consumption. There are plenty of folks who are perfectly happy to pick up a plastic-wrapped container of chicken breasts at the grocery store, but that's not how we do things here at *A Taste of Heaven*."

Sophia wondered if she were the only one cognizant of the fact that he was holding a bloody axe while saying that line.

"The Jefferson Turkey Farm has been in existence for over fifty years. They still employ the same sound practices for raising turkeys they have been following for decades. Today's challenge is two-fold. One, the contestants must kill, butcher, clean, and section their turkeys. And two, they must prepare a delicious meal with a whole turkey provided by the Jefferson Farm." Mr. Smith rubbed his hands together.

Surprisingly Elliott laughed. In fact, Elliott looked completely relaxed.

The other contestants did not look thrilled, although Helene had a small half-smile on her face.

"So here's the schedule for today. First, you butcher your turkeys. Two per pair. Both chefs must help to complete this task."

Poor Chef Herman gagged again. Sophia imagined the producers would either mask the sound in editing, or highlight his discomfort for the show.

"And then you cook. Since the turkeys need to rest after

butchering, we will be giving you a whole bird that has already been soaked in brine for forty-eight hours. You will prepare these for the judges back at our courtyard kitchen. Judges table today will include not only Tarquin, Jonathan, and Jenny, but also all of the eliminated chefs." He waved at the audience.

Sophia saw stark relief etched on their faces. They were probably thrilled they'd already been kicked off the show.

Mr. Smith continued, "You have the option to work with the whole bird or to section it into parts. Any questions?"

"Can I butcher more than two?" Elliott asked. He lifted an axe from the pile on the table, hefting its weight in his hands.

The rest of the contestants laughed nervously, but Sophia realized he was completely serious.

Elliott turned to the farmer. "Have these been sharpened recently?"

"Of course. It's the most humane way to kill the turkeys."

Elliott nodded. "Good." He set the axe down and returned to his place next to Sophia. "Don't worry, sweet. I'll take care of the worst part. Just watch me as I butcher the bird. You can copy what I do. It isn't so bad."

"I can do that part. It's the…"

"The killing. Leave that to me." He cocked his head to the side and Sophia heard it crack.

"Um, I have a question." Nathan raised his hand.

"Yes, Nathan." Mr. Smith was busy wiping his hands with the linen handkerchief.

"Um, how do we get the turkeys? Like…get them. You know?"

All of the contestants turned to watch the turkeys running free in the pen. And eight light bulbs went off at the same time.

Elliott laughed. A loud, booming, diabolical laugh.

"You have to capture the bird," the farmer answered. "Then bring it over here to butcher." He pointed to the stumps lined up in front of them. "Watch out for the talons. There are gloves for you to use."

"Mon Dieu!" Helene grimaced.

"By the way"—Mr. Smith shot an evil smile at the chefs— "you'll be timed for this. The first pair to catch, kill, and butcher their two turkeys will have forty-five extra minutes for this challenge. Second fastest will have twenty extra minutes. Third fastest will have ten extra minutes. And the slowest team has no extra time."

Chef Johnson groaned.

"And one more thing. This is a double elimination. Two pairs are going home today. And the last two pairs will be participating in our final challenge!"

Chef Baldwin whispered, "Fuck."

Elliott smiled.

"You're enjoying this, aren't you?" Sophia asked her partner.

"I'm not afraid to get my hands dirty. I'm not afraid of a little blood and guts. I'm not some pampered prima donna chef." He turned to her and held out his hands. "This is who I am, Sophia. The real me."

"I think there are many facets to *the real you*. But right now, I'm blessedly happy one of those facets can kill turkeys. So I don't have to."

"You're welcome, sweet." He leaned closer to her and whispered in her ear. "And thank you for last night."

She ignored him. He was taunting her. What a time to bring that up!

All of the chefs put on the gloves. Covered with rusty stains that Sophia would rather not think about.

"All right, contestants. The clock will start ticking as soon as I wave the flag." Mr. Smith picked up the little blue and white flag. "Are you ready?"

Only one voice answered. Elliott's voice. "Hell, yeah. Let's get crackin'."

The flag went down, and Elliott took off. He didn't even bother with the gate to the pen. He hopped over the fence and began to chase the turkeys. One down, grabbed by its throat.

Sophia and the others raced to the pen.

"Stay out there, Sophia. I've got this!" Elliott yelled as he grabbed another bird, crushing its throat in his hands. He hopped back over the fence and raced to the stumps. Sophia followed.

She glanced over her shoulder. Chef Baldwin was shouting expletives at Kevin. He had one bird in his arms, but it was twisting and turning. Helene had one slumped in her fist. And Brian and Herman were chasing the birds without success.

Whomp!

Sophia's snapped her gaze back to the butchering area just as Elliott smashed a turkey's head against the side of the barn. He held the other bird tightly against his chest and the stunned one got lowered onto the stump. With one booted foot holding the bird in place, he lifted an axe and cleanly sliced through the neck.

"One down."

She watched, in equal parts horror and respect, as Elliott stunned and decapitated the other bird. She became vaguely aware of the crew and farmhands and past contestants cheering. Someone started to chant *BEAST*, and it caught on like wildfire.

BEAST!

BEAST!

BEAST!

She was appalled, but Elliott just smiled.

And when he was done, two turkey heads lay at his feet, and two birds were ready to be butchered. Chef Baldwin was struggling with one turkey while his partner continued to run around the pen. Helene had one decapitated, but had to return for another.

Sophia shook her head to clear it. She didn't have time to think about the death. To think about the bird, still warm from the chase, heart pumping out the last bit of blood. The bird lying at her feet. Elliott needed her now. She took a deep breath and leaned over to collect the bloody parts.

"What should I do?" she asked, trying to control her trembling limbs.

"Let's get these to the worktable. You okay?" His voice was gentle. A gentle beast.

"Fine," she answered. "Hurry. I want to win." Her voice was shaking.

"Try not to think about it, Sophia. They're not pets. You can't get attached. They're food. Butchering animals properly is a skill. You show respect to the life sacrificed by killing efficiently and excellent preparation. Understand?"

His expression was sympathetic but firm.

"Yes." She nodded. She could do this.

He shot her a look filled with pride. She refused to be the squeamish woman on set.

She dumped the birds on the table. "What now?"

"Watch me. Copy me." He dunked the birds into pots of scalding water and held them under for about a minute.

"This will make the plucking easier," he explained.

He showed her how to de-feather the birds. And then the fun part started. Disemboweling the turkey by slicing open the abdomen. Out came the intestines, the gizzard, the liver. Sophia copied him exactly as she worked on her bird. Out came the heart, the lungs. Elliott showed her how to remove the windpipe and esophagus. She followed him like a robot, ignoring the gore and the stench. They hosed down their birds to cool them off and clean the carcass, then they cut off the feet.

She refused to gag. She barreled through the butchering, keeping up with Elliott step-by-step. This was beyond sickening, but she would not let him down. A vision of her sweet garden popped into her head, and she longed for the feel of seedlings and soil. This challenge might just push her over the edge to vegetarianism.

"How you doing, Sprite? Are you feeling faint?" Elliott tossed the feet into a garbage bin.

"Don't stop. I can do this." She shuddered as her hand

touched something slimy and red on the table. "We're going to win this part. Hurry."

"You're doing great. Poor Johnson is spending more time coddling his partner than completing the challenge. You're impressing the hell out of me, Sophia. And everyone else, too."

She glanced at the audience and was surprised to see them cheering for her and her partner.

She swung her gaze back to the bird. "What's next?" She was anxious to finish.

"Time to section the poultry." Elliott handed her a medium-sized machete, and he grabbed the largest one.

Whack! She followed his lead. Fast, efficient, clean. Wings off, sliced into sections. Legs removed, cut into thigh and drumstick. Breast sliced off, and split into halves. Elliott removed the back meat, too. They loaded up on the parts in a pan. Side-by-side, splattered with blood, Elliott and Sophia finished their task.

He tossed the last piece of meat into the pan, ran over, and rang the "finished" bell.

The other contestants were far behind. They had crushed the competition.

The audience for *A Taste of Heaven* was out of their minds. Cheering, yelling, shocked by their performance.

Elliott grabbed Sophia's hand it held it over their heads in victory. The audience chanted *"Beauty and the Beast!"* and he laughed with abandon. It was the first time Sophia had seen him so relaxed and confident.

They looked like a couple of serial killers. Covered with blood and bits of flesh.

But Elliott was smiling. A brilliant smile, showing off those bright white teeth and genuine joy for a job well-done. His indigo eyes found hers and flashed with triumph.

Elliott Adamson had just gotten his mojo back.

She waved their arms in the air and shouted with the audience.

He turned to her. "Now we discuss our menu. I plan to

win today. We will be in the finals tomorrow."

Sophia laughed. "Don't you want to clean up first?"

He looked down at his gore-spattered uniform. "Yeah. That's probably a good idea." He chuckled. "You were fantastic. And I know that wasn't easy for you."

"Thank you for mentoring me. I just followed your lead. You were a natural."

His expression turned serious. "It's the cycle of life. I guess I'm good at the basics. Like killing things."

She stepped closer to him. "You're good at many things, Chef Adamson. And what you just accomplished was skillful and fearless. You have no idea how much I admire that."

"Thank you," he answered softly. "Let's get cleaned up. I have some ideas for dinner." He removed his gloves. "But I want to know *your* ideas, too. Today we cook as a team. The team to beat. Got it?"

She nodded, and they ran to a washroom in the main building.

🍂 🍂 🍂

"Time to talk turkey, Chef Brown. It should come as no surprise that I like a traditional preparation."

Elliott leaned against their worktable in the Vermont Culinary Institute kitchen and scribbled in his notebook.

He was different today. More relaxed. The tension had eased out of his joints with each slam of the axe, each slice of the machete. As crew members came over to congratulate him and joke about his beastly performance, he issued them a genuine smile.

And when the inevitable *"Beauty and the Beast"* reference was made, he turned to Sophia and laughed. "I told you they were going to say that."

He wasn't in the slightest bit upset. In fact, he seemed to revel in this new role on the show. A beast from Scotland— driven, angry, talented. Fierce. And Sophia was no longer the pretty little doll or the garden fairy with a wreath of flowers in her hair. She'd been right next to him the whole time. Hacking, butchering. Blood-soaked and victorious.

Now came the real test. Could Sophia and Elliott find some middle ground and cook a meal together? If not, this would be the end of the line for both of them.

"What is a traditional Scottish preparation for turkey? Do you cook that for Christmas?"

"Aye. Also roast goose from time to time. But my turkey recipe is fantastic."

"Tell me, Elliott. Do we have enough time?"

He nodded. "Absolutely. Especially since we won the extra minutes." He winked at her and she laughed.

"Yes, we did, *Beast*. So what's on the menu?"

"We soak prunes in whisky and tea, dip them in honey, and stuff them with walnuts. These are mixed with sausage for the stuffing. I usually soak the prunes for several days, but we'll make do."

"My God. That sounds fabulous."

Elliott nodded, but said nothing. He was staring at her intently.

"And…"

"And…"

What was he waiting for? He started to fiddle with the pencil.

Finally she realized he was waiting for her input! He had no idea how to banter back-and-forth or to brainstorm creatively.

She broke the awkward silence. "Elliott, are you waiting for my suggestions for dinner?"

"Aye. I'm waiting."

"I think…we should go with the honey."

"I use heather honey in North Berwick. But I'm sure the honey here will be fine."

"My favorite is from the Akins Apiary. They have delicious

apple honey. It's rare, but I'll see if they have some in the pantry."

"Excellent. What...what else do you like about the honey?"

Sophia tried not to laugh out loud at Elliott's stilted and awkward attempt at conversation. The give-and-take was clearly not a natural process for him.

"Let's use the honey in all our dishes. How about roasted vegetables in a balsamic-honey dressing? With thyme? I think rutabaga and turnips would be a nice side for the turkey."

He scratched something on his tablet. "Keep going."

"And how about a bitter green salad? Maybe arugula and dandelion greens with a honey vinaigrette. That will cut the richness of the bird."

Elliott nodded. "I like both of those ideas. This meal will showcase the best of both of us...a traditional Scottish roast bird and various preparations for the vegetables and greens. Let's search the pantry and see if we can find that honey." He cleared his throat nervously. "Sophia."

She waited for him to continue. She ached for him, the strained look on his face.

"I know...I haven't been the easiest partner. I want you to know I appreciate that you chose my *amuse-bouche* the first day. I appreciate that you've put up with me and my less-than-stellar personality." He shrugged. "I appreciate all of it, sweet." She knew exactly what he was thinking about at that moment, and it wasn't cooking.

"And I appreciate your talent, your fearlessness, your devotion to Scottish tradition. Let's make this meal sing. We can do it." She smiled at him and hoped it was reassuring.

He leaned over and kissed her on the side of the face. Half-way on the skin just beneath her ear. And partly on the lobe. And before he moved away from her, he bit her. Gently.

"Don't even think about it, Adamson."

"I deserved that for decapitating the birds."

"We have a job to do. Focus."

"I'm pretty damned good at multi-tasking, Sophia."

She narrowed her eyes at his wholly innocent expression. "Behave yourself, Elliott."

"I haven't behaved myself since I was a wee laddie. No fun in that."

"Let's look for honey." She tried to ignore him. It was like ignoring a mountain.

Not remotely possible.

The investigation for the honey distracted him and they discovered quite the stash. She collected bottles of amber liquid and he collected mace and walnuts and onion for the stuffing.

As they assembled their ingredients, Sophia heard a high-pitched chirp.

Jenny the Blogger.

"Well, well, well. Look who it is. *Beauty and the Beast*. I think the television viewers are going to eat you two up. With a spoon." Jenny leaned over their table and rested on her elbows. Her blouse gaped open to reveal a sheer bra and two erect nipples.

"Please don't lean on our table. It's unsanitary." Elliott glanced up and looked directly into Jenny's eyes, avoiding the obvious show. "You don't want to get sick on our food, do you?"

"You're joking, right? You served us black pudding, Chef Adamson. I don't think sanitation is an issue."

"What did you think about the turkey farm, Jenny?" Sophia attempted to change the subject before Elliott exploded.

"Disgusting. Absolutely disgusting. I'm not surprised Herman vomited. I wanted to vomit too."

"It's sometimes shocking to see where your turkey cutlet comes from, right?" Elliott continued to chop onions without making eye contact.

"I know exactly where my turkey cutlet comes from. But I

don't think that our viewers are interested in so much graphic detail."

Sophia piped up, "I guess the producers disagree. Or they'll edit that part so it's not so disconcerting."

Jenny shrugged and stood up. "Well, I think the viewers would rather see you picking flowers and herbs in the garden, Mrs. Brown. You're a natural." She smiled at Sophia with less-than-genuine enthusiasm. But at least it wasn't all-out-hostility.

The look she shot Elliott wasn't quite as warm. "And there always has to be a villain on the show, right, Mr. Adamson?"

"That's Chef Adamson, Jenny. I earned that title. Don't forget it."

Jenny clenched her hands, and Sophia wondered if the fake nails hurt as they punctured her skin.

As the blogger walked away, Elliott whistled under his breath. "Twenty bucks says the producers are regretting that decision."

"Just remember, she's judging us today."

"So are a lot of talented chefs. I trust them not to throw us under the bus."

The hours raced by. But Elliott never got flustered. He worked through his checklist in a calm, organized manner. He assembled the stuffing, dressed the turkey, and basted the bird as it roasted. Sophia worked on the vegetables and greens. When she asked Elliott to try her dressing, he nodded. She held up a spoon to his lips.

"Delicious," he said.

The heated look in his eyes made her think about heavy breathing and rocking against a dormitory door.

That single word made Sophia tremble.

A few minutes later, Elliott nudged her with his elbow. "Sophia. Would you…" He held a spoon in his hands.

"What is this?"

"The glaze for the bird. Lots of good whisky in here." His

expression was oddly blank. Unsure. Exposed. Elliott was asking for her approval.

She swallowed the bite. "My God. That is so good. You have a way with sauces, Chef Adamson. And whisky."

"Well, I'm Scottish." He cleared his throat.

This was a big step. He'd trusted her. He'd solicited her opinion. Even if he considered her a lowly serf in his kingdom, he was trying his best.

And when the time finally came to serve their dish, which smelled like heaven and boasted bold, rich flavors, the judges couldn't contain their enthusiasm.

"The *Beast* has outdone himself this time."

The remaining eight contestants watched as their future was decided. It was an odd scenario. Sophia had been judged many times in her life. As a wife, as a mother, as a woman. As a student, as a daughter, as a sister. As a friend. But this was different. As these people shoveled food into their mouths—food that was sustenance for their bodies, art on a plate, uniquely inspired, hopefully satisfying—her future would be decided. Would this really make a difference in her life? Would she return home and fade back into obscurity? Would she become a minor celebrity and offer autographs to strangers?

Would she take a chance and host a television show? Completely change her life? Was she fearless enough to try?

Strangely enough, that option did not appeal. This whole false veneer for the camera was uncomfortable for her. The old dream of opening her own little bistro still lingered, however. In a sweet corner shop, with window boxes and crates of wine and her daughters laughing with her in the kitchen. Could *that* fantasy come true?

And why did that fantasy suddenly include a hulking Scottish chef with poor manners and a chip on his shoulder the size of Loch Ness?

"Well. This was quite the feast." Tarquin patted his lips with a napkin and saluted the remaining chefs. "Well played, ladies and gentlemen."

"We've come full circle," Jonathan said. "From the most elemental part of food preparation—the killing and butchering of an animal—to the elevated and sophisticated presentation of a beautiful meal. I am impressed with what all of you have accomplished in five short days."

Jenny scrunched up her nose. "I'm trying to forget about the first part, Jonathan."

The other judges laughed, but Jonathan didn't crack a smile.

"I did, however, enjoy the second part. These dishes were just divine."

Mr. Smith stood next to the finalists and waved his ridiculous flag. Sophia had a fleeting thought about throwing it into a bonfire.

"And now for the moment of truth. Who will be participating in the finals tomorrow? This is a double elimination. Judges, what do you think?"

Sophia glanced down the line. Baldwin was tense. Kevin looked green. The hipster and his Filipino sidekick were obviously agitated. Helene had her serious face plastered on. Nathan bubbled with excitement. God bless Short Chubby Guy.

The one person whose attitude shocked her the most was Elliott. After the last challenge, she had expected anxiety, hostility, distrust. But today he seemed utterly confident. Cocky.

And Sophia?

She wanted to win.

Even if she refused the television show. Even if she never opened that bistro. She wanted to win to show everyone that she could. She could do this.

And she wanted to win for Elliott.

Jonathan stood at the table and raised his wine glass. "I would like to make a toast to the first partnership that finally...meshed." He sipped his Zinfandel. "I wondered how long it would take. How long for two strangers to learn to complement each other on the plate? Was it possible to do in a week?

I know chefs who have worked for years with partners and were never able to accomplish this feat. It's tricky. That's one of the reasons I agreed to judge for *A Taste of Heaven*. This premise fascinates me."

Tarquin also stood. "I agree with Chef Rutgers. There are many times in your culinary career you need to work as a team. It's not always about you, your desires, your talent. Sometimes cooking requires compromise. And as we all know, a chef's ego may not handle that too well."

That elicited quite a few chuckles from the table.

Jenny the Blogger pushed her curls behind a shoulder. "I'm a firm believer in team work. My family is my team. I love to cook with my children. They are the first to point out my flaws. Gently." She winked at the camera. "And they are also the first to pat me on the back when I do something creative and inspired. I love my team."

For the first time, Sophia actually felt connected to Jenny. That sentiment hadn't been forced for the taping. It was genuine and sweet, and it made Sophia like the blogger a bit more.

Sophia's daughters were her team, too.

Mr. Smith faced the eight finalists. "So, judges, who finally did it? Who meshed today? Let's find out who our winner is, and then we can deal with the final pair."

Sophia felt like vomiting. She couldn't control the tremor in her limbs.

Elliott pressed his arm—hot and hairy and familiar—against her elbow and whispered, "*Steady.*"

Chef Rutgers stepped in front of the contestants and swung his gaze from one end of the line to the other. He nodded slightly. Then he approached Elliott and held out his hand. "Chef Adamson. Congratulations."

Elliott bowed his head and released a long hiss of breath. A hiss filled with desperation and hope, fear of failure. Courage. And relief.

He shook hands with Jonathan and his eyes flashed with triumph. Then he turned to Sophia and smiled.

She grabbed onto his hand and wouldn't let go.

They'd done it! They made it into the finals!

Jonathan continued. "I know this hasn't been easy for you, Elliott. But you dazzled us today. The turkey butchering was damned impressive. The traditional Scottish preparation of the bird was brilliant. Packed with flavor. And Sophia." He patted her knuckles. "Your sides paired perfectly with Elliott's turkey. The honey-inspired recipes were delicious. You are a wonderful amateur cook."

"As well as a diplomatic and thoughtful partner," Tarquin added. "Right, Elliott? She tamed the *Beast*." He laughed.

Elliott nodded. "I'm a lucky man. She was the perfect partner for me."

His eyes blazed at her and she felt light-headed.

"Yes, you are lucky, Elliott. Good to know you recognize that." Jenny didn't look quite as impressed as the other judges. "I loved the stuffing and the beautiful salad. And your turkey was perfectly cooked…moist and delicious. Well done to the both of you."

Mr. Smith handed each of them a ticket. "Here are your tickets to the finals. You made it! Congratulations. You may go stand next to the garden."

Elliott and Sophia walked to the garden, still hand-in-hand, both trembling. The edge of the perennial border was buzzing with hummingbirds in the dusk. Elliott released her hand and crushed her in his arms.

"Sophia. *Sophia*." His voice was barely more than a whisper.

She buried her face in his neck, warm and comforting. He smelled like honey. "We did it," she answered softly.

He pulled back and raked his gaze over her face. "Yes, we did. How about that?"

The two of them laughed quietly. Afraid to make noise and breach this perfect moment.

"Christ. I honestly can't believe it. The damned blogger hates me."

"But she loved our meal today. They all did. We finally pulled it together." Sophia shook her head, still feeling slightly bewildered.

"I've never done this before," Elliott said. "The give-and-take, the compromise…the listening. I wasn't kidding when I said you were the perfect partner for me, Sophia. You were patient and understanding."

"We worked as a team, and you survived to tell the tale. How about that?" she teased.

He chuckled. "Aye."

"So how do you feel?"

"Honestly? Scared shitless."

She laughed. "Why?"

"I'm used to being a monarch. In a kingdom of one. Just me. Alone. Allowing someone else to have input is completely foreign to me."

"We make a good team." Sophia realized that statement was heavy with meaning, and she waited to see how Elliott would react.

He nodded. "Aye, we do. I guess an old dog can learn some new tricks after all. Or maybe a *beast*."

Before she could answer, they heard shouting at the judges' table.

"Pomegranate syrup is the perfect complement for turkey." Chef Johnson's voice cracked as he argued his point.

"Perhaps, if executed properly. But this lacked flavor and punch." Tarquin raised a brow at the red-faced chef.

They continued to quarrel, as the chefs defended their choices, their meals, their chance to remain in the competition. In the end, Brian and Herman were released. And sadly Helene and her partner Nathan, as well. Sophia was disappointed to see them go. She liked Helene and her French sensibilities, her sense of fair play.

And that left Michael Baldwin and his struggling partner from North Carolina.

If Michael was trying to establish a sexy lothario image, it certainly wasn't working for Sophia. Yes, he was handsome in a classic way, flirtatious for the camera, and serious about the competition. But he lacked the passion for his cuisine that Elliott and Helene, and even Lin Lin shared. If she'd ever met Michael in the real world, she would have dismissed him right away. There was something about Chef Baldwin she didn't trust. And yet the ornery Scot had won her over.

They called the finalist pairs to the judging table and the cast and crew honored them with a round of applause. Elliott lifted Sophia's hand above his head and the audience cheered *"Beast!"*

How about that? The villain of the show had turned into Fan Favorite.

Sophia was delighted.

 Chapter Sixteen

S ophia attempted to plump the flat, dejected pillow on her metal bed. She would be relieved to be home in a few days.

Wouldn't she?

Of course she would. Back home. Back with the girls.

Of course she would.

A rap on the door startled her.

He wouldn't.

She opened the door.

He would.

"Hello, sweet. Guess who?" Elliott lifted a bottle of cheap champagne and two plastic cups.

"You have got to be kidding me. It's late, Elliott. Go to bed. We have a big day tomorrow."

She started to shut her door, but his big booted foot jammed the way.

"Oh, no, you don't. We're celebrating tonight. We made

it to the finals. Come on, join me for just one glass of bubbly." Elliott was certainly in a playful mood. That made her nervous.

"Tomorrow is the final challenge. We both need to sleep."

"We'll sleep. After."

Her eyes narrowed. "After…what?"

"After we drink this shitty champagne." He shot her an amused look.

"Classy, Elliott. I like the plastic cups."

"Thank you, Sprite. I do what I can." He poured the champagne and offered her a cup.

"Shall we toast?" He held his glass close to her.

"Okay. You have five minutes. I'm too old to drink and stay up all night. I need to be rested for the finals. You may be able to run around and butcher turkeys without a second thought, but I need my wits about me for tomorrow." She took a sip and grimaced. "Dear God, this is awful." She shook her head. "Anyway, Michael won't just roll over and play dead. We're going to have to bring our A-game to beat him."

"Bah!" Elliott waved a hand through the air. "Don't insult me. That bastard is a burger-flipper."

"Hmm." She took another sip, and then set the cup down on her dresser. "Do you want to tell me why you hate Chef Baldwin so much? What is your history?"

"He's an asshole."

"Care to elaborate?"

Elliott released a huge sigh. "A long time ago, I took a cooking workshop with a bunch of up-and-coming chefs. Baldwin was there."

"And?"

"And he thought he was Mr. Hot Shit. Mr. American Chef. He'd just graduated from the CIA, and he was convinced he was the next best thing."

"I would imagine a lot of new chefs feel that way."

"True. But usually you need something to back that up. I won the *Best New Chef* award in the UK when I got out of school. I worked for various master chefs in Edinburgh before branching out on my own. Baldwin is one of those guys who thinks good looks and charisma will earn him respect. No one gives a shit about that. Maybe if you're on TV. But in the kitchen, only one thing counts. Your cooking. *The. End.*"

"This still doesn't explain your deep hatred for the man." Sophia took the empty plastic cup from Elliott's hands and tossed it into the trash. "What did he do to you?"

"He mocked Scottish food. He has no appreciation for anything outside of his little American world. It drove me crazy then. It drives me crazy now."

He stroked a rough finger down the side of Sophia's cheek and she struggled not to shiver.

"I understand that folks might not understand a culture outside of their own. But if you're a modern-day chef, you show respect. Even if you don't eat it. Even if you don't cook it. You still show respect."

"You don't respect his American cooking."

Elliott laughed. "That's because he cooks diner food. I have a ton of respect for Chef Rutgers. He might be old school, but the man is extremely talented."

Elliott tugged on Sophia's hand and pulled her down on the creaky bed.

"What do you think you're up to, Chef Adamson?" She suppressed a sigh as he kissed her neck.

"Attempting to seduce my partner. She's a prickly little thing."

He kissed her ear lobe.

"Maybe she's trying to keep this professional."

The bed creaked as he ran his lips over her collarbone. Sophia swayed.

"Maybe she needs to lighten up."

"What are your intentions, if you don't mind me asking?"

Elliott smirked. "You sound so very old-fashioned, sweet. All right. How about this—a fuck for good luck?"

Sophia burst out laughing. "A good luck fuck?"

Elliott nodded. "Yep. A good luck fuck." The bed creaked again as he pinned her with his arms.

"Are you insane?"

"No, I'm horny. I can't stop thinking about you."

"That's plainly evident." His erection pulsed against her pajama pants which gave Sophia a little thrill.

"Hasn't anyone ever told you sex is a great stress-reliever?" he asked.

Sophia giggled. The bed made a grating noise. "We cannot have sex in this bed, Elliott. Everyone in the entire dorm will know what we're up to. This bed sounds like it's about to fall apart."

Elliott made a few exploratory grinding motions, and the squeaking noises made both of them laugh.

"Okay, the bed's out." He stood up and grabbed her hand. "We'll do it against the wall. It worked out pretty nicely with the door episode."

"What?" Her eyes grew wide as Elliott Adamson pressed her against the wall.

"Wrap your arms around my neck."

"Oh, no. No way."

"Do it, woman!"

She laughed softly as he lifted her in his arms. So much for professional behavior. Her curiosity about sex with Elliott Adamson was about to be appeased.

"Oh, yeah, that's what I'm talking about." He rocked against her pelvis. "Do you feel that, sweetheart? All that Scottish knob for you."

Sophia buried her face in Elliott's neck and laughed until her stomach ached. "Well, to be honest, I was a little bit disappointed with the door episode."

He stopped rocking. "What? Why? I got your rockets off, didn't I?"

"We skipped too many bases. You skipped first base, and second base, and half of third base…"

"What are you talking about? What bases?"

"Oh, I forgot. You Scots probably don't get the baseball analogy."

"Educate me, love."

"It must be an American thing. Using baseball as an analogy for sex. First base is…kissing."

"Snogging," he said as he nuzzled her lips.

"Um, yes. Second base is…" She blushed. Embarrassingly. Elliott lifted a brow. "Yesssssss?"

"Um, copping a feel. You know. Under a woman's blouse."

"A nice grope. Okay. What's next?"

"Third base. Sneaking into each other's pants. So to speak."

"This dirty talk is getting me randy. I can't wait to hear about the next base."

"A home run. It means—"

"Ahhhhh. Let me guess. A shag for the win. Am I right?" She giggled. "Aye."

Elliott frowned. "I apologize for rushing the other night. And skipping these important bases. I'll make sure to include them all today."

"Good idea. Skipping bases is frowned upon. What kind of baseball game is that?" She shot him a cheeky look.

He growled at her.

"You Americans are fucking obsessed with baseball." Elliott kissed her.

Oh! It was glorious. The brush of his beard, the softness of his lips. And his tongue, that sneaked into her mouth and got her hot and panting and breathless.

He lowered her feet to the ground and they kissed and kissed and kissed until Sophia was convinced the most delicious thing on earth was Elliott and cheap champagne.

"First base down," he whispered.

She shivered as he ran his tongue along the shell of her ear. He unbuttoned her pajama top and cupped her breasts. Gently squeezed and pinched and finally sucked her nipples until her legs gave out and she slid down the wall onto the floor.

He followed her down and devoured her. Licking and squeezing with the utmost enthusiasm. She had love-bites all over her chest.

"Damn, you're pretty, Sophia." He kissed the tip of her nose and smiled at her drunken expression. "Second base down."

And after he slid off her pants, and his pants, they finally rounded third base for both parties. Hands crawling over skin, with gentle touches and secret discoveries. He bunched up his sweatshirt under her back, attempting to make her more comfortable. And when he slid home, nestled deep inside of her, she wished the game would go on forever.

Who was this Sophia? The good little widow, the well-behaved doll, was scraping her nails along Elliott Adamson's bollocks and making him groan with lust. She stroked them and squeezed them and kissed them until she begged her for mercy. Who was this woman?

A woman unafraid. He made her that way.

At least for one night.

So she took his breath and his slickness and his touch. She took him into her body. She took her pleasure. In a most selfish way, quite unlike the old Sophia. And he gloried in it.

His smile lit her up. She'd had casual sex before. For God's sake, she was forty-seven years old. But this thing they were doing wasn't a "good luck fuck." This thing—with his indigo eyes, intense and watchful, gazing down at her—was something more than that.

After he'd emptied himself into her with a shout and a collection of impressive Scottish expletives that were certainly heard all over the dorm, he carried her to the bed. Surprisingly, it didn't collapse under their weight. He held her in his arms, and they slept. When the purple sunrise appeared outside, she discovered he was awake.

"Winning day," he said.

 Chapter
Seventeen

S ophia knew something was wrong the minute she walked
onto the set the next morning. Instead of an atmosphere
of anticipation, the kitchen swarmed with worried-look-
ing producers and frantic crew members. Lights flickered on
and off, and half of the kitchen was shadowed in darkness.

Elliott was tense. His impatience to get started was
palpable.

"What's going on?" he snapped.

"I don't know. Mr. Smith doesn't look happy."

They both grimaced as Harold slid across the room in his
penny loafers.

"Hard to imagine that man in running shoes, isn't it?"
Elliott raised a brow.

"That's not very nice, Elliott. He's doing the best he can."

"I don't trust him. I don't trust anyone here. Except you."
Elliott's eyes narrowed as he scanned the room. "Great. Here
comes Lancelot and Mr. Barbecue."

Michael and Kevin joined them.

Chef Baldwin jerked his head toward the cluster of producers. "What do you think is going on? Any ideas?"

"None," Elliott answered. "But I'm ready to cook. I hope they figure this out in a hurry."

"Me too," said Kevin. "I can't believe we made it this far!" He smiled nervously at Sophia, and she wanted to pat his head. He was like an overeager puppy, and she had no doubt that Michael treated him accordingly.

Mr. Smith held up his hands. "I have an announcement. I'm sorry to tell you this, but we will not be having our final taping today."

Elliott growled low in his throat.

"We are having some electrical issues with our kitchen. Until everything is repaired, we're on temporary break. I've been told the delay will only be twenty-four hours, which I'm praying is true, since we're on a tight schedule and a tight budget." He wiped his forehead and stuffed the used linen into his pants pocket. "In the meantime, the finalists will have the day off. We'll give you a voucher for meals and other expenses. Feel free to explore Vermont, relax, sleep. Tomorrow, if all goes well, we will be taping our final segment."

Michael shook his head in disgust. "Is this some sort of psychological warfare? Getting us hyped up and then leaving us hanging?"

Mr. Smith blanched. "No. Of course not. Believe me, I'm not happy about the delay either. This has been a very intense and rushed schedule, so it's probably just as well to have a short break. Don't knock it, Baldwin."

Elliott's arms were crossed tightly. Sophia tapped his elbow.

"What?" he barked.

"We have the day off. Don't look so glum."

"I want to get this bloody contest over with. I want to win. I want my big fat check and to head home to Scotland and fix the mess I'm in." He hissed at her with impatience.

Sophia was surprised to feel an ache in her chest when he spoke of leaving the country.

"I know you do, but there's nothing we can do about this now. Let's go."

"Where the hell are we going? To our rooms?" Elliott's foul mood was escalating.

"No. We're going home. To *my* home. I live about fifteen minutes from here. We're going to spend the day dawdling in the garden and sipping lemonade and hanging out with my daughters. And tomorrow you'll be refreshed and ready to go."

"I don't work that way. I don't need to be…*refreshed*."

Sophia laughed. "Oh, Elliott. You look so put-upon. Lighten up."

She grabbed his hand and pulled him toward the parking lot.

They were going on a field trip.

Twenty-five years ago, when David had been offered a job at Patterson College in Vermont, she'd trailed along to investigate a potential new home. Their truck had bounced on a raggedy dirt road, and they'd turned into a driveway made of rocks. The cottage was sweet. Small. Needed some work. But Sophia hardly noticed.

She'd been focused solely on the vista behind the little house—mountains covered with evergreens and fields of wildflowers. Tall purple lupine leaned gently in the breeze. Wild chicory and Indian paintbrush framed the side of the road. And nestled beneath a dense copse of maple were wild blackberry bushes. She meandered over, plucked fruits off the shrubs and popped them into her mouth, as David discussed mortgages with the real estate man.

When David had asked her what she thought, she said, "Surprisingly sweet. Delicious." He laughed.

"The house, Sophia. What do you think about the house?"

She'd glanced at the porch, which appeared to be hanging on by a thread, and said, "Yes." That was all.

Every year they'd worked on a project. A new porch. An updated kitchen. Built-in shelves in the living room for David's extensive book collection. Window seats for the girls' bedrooms. Sophia started with plantings in front of the house, and graduated to perennial borders and a vegetable patch. She'd attempted Forget-Me-Not seeds one year, and they'd spread all over the lawn. And every spring, when mud season was making her yank out her hair, the backyard became a carpet of delicate blue flowers. She and the girls would spread a blanket for a picnic, speaking in whispers so they didn't disturb the Spring Fairies. Sophia baked sugar cookies drizzled with powdered sugar frosting and topped with candied violets.

The girls grew up, and the tricycles in the driveway were replaced with backpacks straining at the seams and hidden packs of cigarettes, and eventually the house became empty for months at a time. It was heavy with anticipation, like a puppy with his wet nose pressed against the window, waiting for the girls to come home. Sophia and David continued with their life and their activities, but the quiet was sometimes oppressive and melancholy.

Sophia tried to pack the quiet holes with plants. She'd arrive home from the nursery with flats of Johnny Jump-Ups and thorny roses and delicate ferns. David joked they could charge admission when guests arrived at their house since it was beginning to resemble a botanical garden.

Those holes were bittersweet, but not utterly crushing, because the day would come when the rusty Honda crunched on the rocky drive and the dented Subaru slid into the remaining spot, and all the holes would be filled up again and Sophia could breathe a long, sweet sigh of relief.

And then a new hole blasted into her life. The hole that could never be filled up.

The hole that shocked the hell out of her. Not because it was so unexpected, which it was. Because it was so destructive. She hadn't realized that those quiet moments, the ones that seemed so unimportant, were the threads of her life holding everything together. Holding herself together.

And when they unraveled, so did she.

She turned and watched Elliott stare out the window. He vibrated with anger. He had no interest in a day of relaxation. He was ready to work. He grumbled and complained bitterly about the change in schedule. She'd stopped asking him questions, since every response was pithy and terse. Just a few short hours ago he was mellow and aroused. Now he was snapping at her. The man was exasperating.

Her truck dipped and crested on the dirt road as they flew by familiar scenery. The farm stand at the corner. Mr. Miller's horses in the field across the street. August was a lazy time in Vermont. Insects buzzed around the overgrown grasses and frogs croaked among the *Nymphaea*, and the girls, when they were home, sat on the front porch with their coffee cups in the morning and chatted with the neighbors who walked by. They wore tattered college sweatshirts and baggy pajamas and just the sound of their voices through the window settled Sophia's heart. Made the racing beat slow down and the small tremors in her hands subside.

She pulled into her driveway and glanced at the house. Painted a fresh coat of coconut white with a red tin roof and flower boxes at every window, her fix-it-up cottage now looked like the quintessential Vermont dwelling. Bicycles leaned against the garage door, and a wheelbarrow filled with compost was parked next to the shed. She saw her daughters on the porch, and Sophia laughed with happiness.

"We're home," she announced and Elliott grunted. "Be nice, Grumpy Scottish Bastard."

"Worried I'll snap at your daughters?"

"No, I'm worried they'll snap at you if your manners don't improve."

He raised his brow at that comment.

"Mom!" Cady yanked open her door. "What happened? Did you win? Did you lose?"

"Who's this?" Emilia asked, staring at Elliott with undisguised curiosity.

Sophia stepped from the car and hugged Cady, perhaps with a bit too much enthusiasm.

"Mommy, is everything okay?" Cady peered over her shoulder. "That guy looks sort of pissed off."

Sophia laughed. "Elliott, why don't you get out of the car so I can introduce you? Hmm?"

He rolled his eyes and stomped over to her side. "Let me guess. Your daughters. They look exactly like you."

"Your powers of observation are astounding."

"Thank you, madam. I do try."

The girls watched the interplay and giggled.

"I haven't won or lost…yet. The competition isn't over. We have the day off due to technical difficulties on the set."

Elliott scratched his beard. "Yes, evidently we can't cook in the dark. So here we are."

Sophia squeezed his arm. "This is Chef Elliott Adamson from North Berwick, Scotland. He's my partner for the challenges."

"You have a partner? I didn't see that in the description." Cady inspected Elliott from head to toe.

Sophia nodded. "I know. It was a surprise. The producers paired an amateur cook with a professional for the duration of the competition. Elliott and I made it to the finals, which should be tomorrow."

"Mom!" Emilia shouted and flung her arms around Sophia's neck. "I'm so proud of you. I knew you could do it."

Cady snuggled into their embrace.

Elliott looked amused. "By the way, girls, if you breathe a word of this to anyone, you'll be tarred and feathered and left out as feed at the Jefferson Turkey Farm. We signed paperwork to that effect. The producers want to keep all of this a big secret until the show airs. Understand?"

"Of course." Emilia nodded. "We would never do anything to hurt your chances in the competition."

Sophia slid her arm around Em's waist. "Elliott, this is Daughter Number One."

He smiled at Sophia. And then he chuckled and shook his head. "Ah, Sophia, you are a treasure. Daughter Number One is Emilia. Am I right?"

Em smirked. "Yep."

"And this is Daughter Number Two."

Elliott held out his hand for both girls. "The artsy-fartsy one, Cady."

Cady giggled. "That's how you described me? Artsy-fartsy?"

Em elbowed her in the waist. "Fartsy, for sure."

"Girls. Enough. We need to entertain Elliott for twenty-four hours. He's very anxious about the finals tomorrow."

"I'm not anxious. I just want to get it over with, win, get my money, and head home."

Emilia and Cady laughed.

Elliott looked at the cottage. "What a swell little spot. Flowers and hummingbirds and a rocker on the porch. It sort of makes me want to…" He staggered and pretended to pass out. "Fall asleep."

"Oh my God. Mom, has he been like this the whole time?" Cady asked.

"Pretty much. He's in an especially bad mood today. Worse than normal, I think. He wasn't happy about the delay in taping."

"So, Mr. Adamson—" Emilia said.

"—that's *Chef* Adamson," Elliott answered.

Cady hung her head and tried to muffle her laughter.

Emilia's eyebrows rose to her hairline. "*Chef* Adamson. What do you like to do? We have bikes and a kayak and—"

"I cook."

Cady snickered. "You cook? That's a big shocker. You're a chef."

Elliott shot her a frosty look. "Sophia, your girls have inherited your sarcasm."

"Yes, they have."

"Chef Adamson, do you do anything other than cook?" Emilia looked genuinely interested in his response.

"No."

"No?"

"That's what I said." Elliott leaned against the car and glanced at his watch. "How much longer?"

"Holy crap, he is so freakin' rude!" Cady tugged on Sophia's sleeve and whispered into her ear. "Is he driving you crazy?"

Sophia kissed her cheek. "Nope. I'm used to him now," she answered. Had she really only known Elliott for five days? Why did it feel like forever?

Emilia cocked her head at Elliott. "What do you cook?" she asked.

"Scottish food."

"Like…haggis?" Cady's eyes grew huge.

"Like haggis. Your mother told me I can prepare some for you this evening. I know you're going to love it."

Cady and Emilia screamed in unison.

"Is he joking about that, Mom?" Emilia said.

"He is joking." She turned to Elliott and sighed. "I'm sure the last thing you want to do on your day off is—"

"Wrong. It's the only thing I want to do. Cooking relaxes me. What else am I going to do today?" Elliott looked at the cottage and frowned.

"Really?" Sophia was shocked.

"Really."

"Well, if Chef Adamson is interested, the Woodstock Farmer's Market is open all day on the green. We could load up there with some fresh fruits and veggies—" Cady said.

"Christ. Just like your mum. How about proteins?"

Cady grimaced. "Sure. There is organic beef, a fish monger, several dairies with eggs and cheese…"

"Let's go."

"You're quite the conversationalist, Chef Adamson. The producers must love you on that show."

Emilia made the comment with a totally straight face, but Sophia could tell she was about to burst into laughter.

Elliott answered without missing a beat. "My nickname is *Beast*."

Cady gasped. "You're joking, right?"

"No. And your mum is Beauty, of course. We're the pair to beat, right Sophia?"

"We're the pair who's going to win."

"Mom." Emilia's eyes filled with tears. "I'm so happy for you. You sound…different."

Cady squeezed Sophia again. "Em's right. You sound better. Happier. More confident."

"Not…lost anymore." Emilia wiped the tears off her cheeks.

Sophia opened her arms, and both girls embraced her, laughing and crying and squeezing her tightly, which surprisingly made her breathe easier. And over the tops of their heads she saw Elliott watching them quietly. He nodded at her, just once, and she closed her eyes in surrender.

✿ ✿ ✿

"No, no, no. Like this." Elliott grabbed Emilia's hand as she stirred tomato sauce in a stainless steel skillet and tried to direct her movements. "You don't beat the shit out of the tomatoes. They've already been crushed, Em. You stir, gently, trying to incorporate the other flavors into the sauce. See?" He released her arm.

Emilia adjusted her stirring technique. "I wasn't aware I was beating the shit out of the tomatoes. I'm going to be arrested for tomato abuse."

"Well, you'll look good in an orange jumpsuit," Cady said. She nibbled on a piece of basil. "Orange is your color."

"True. That." Emilia swirled the sauce in the skillet. "Okay, Beast, what's next?"

Elliott turned to Sophia and sighed. "Are they always this cranky?"

Sophia smiled. "Actually, they're in excellent spirits today. Girls, stop teasing Elliott."

"What?" Cady shook her head. "His name is *Beast*. I think he can take a little bit of ribbing, for God's sake."

Elliott grumbled, but it was all for show. As soon as he'd made himself at home in her kitchen, he'd begun to relax. What an incongruous scene. The big, hulking brute of a Scot surrounded by hanging plants and mismatched teacups, floral tiles, and girly knick-knacks. Every time he barked orders at the girls, they dished it right back. Soon he wasn't even bothering to hide his smiles. Sophia had known this trip would settle him down.

Emilia waved her spoon. "For the record, I think I was being exceedingly gentle with those tomatoes." She leaned over the pot and scooped up a spoonful of sauce. "Here, Mom, try it. Let's see if I *incorporated the flavors*."

Sophia tasted the tomato cream sauce. It was her favorite. Simple, elegant. "This is perfect. And so…not Scottish. How is it that Elliott is preparing this Scottish-free meal? He won't do it for the show."

Elliott shrugged. "The girls told me at the market this is your favorite meal. I decided to thank you for putting up with my crap."

He leaned close enough for Sophia to see the glimmer in his eyes.

"Am I allowed to kiss you, love, or not in front of the kiddies?" He whispered it, challenging her.

"I guess that's up to you. I don't mind."

So he kissed her, accepting the challenge. Only their lips met, touched, lingered for just a moment.

"Oh. My. God." Cady's mouth hung open.

Emilia continued to stir the sauce. "Looks like more than food is cooking on the set of *A Taste of Heaven*."

Sophia shrugged in a totally nonchalant manner. Even though her heart was beating a mile a minute and she struggled to hide her blush.

"Bad pun, Em! Uh, Mom, can I talk to you for a minute. In private?" Cady cocked her head toward the hallway.

"Go ahead, Sophia. I'm sure your daughter wants to pump you for information. About the Beast. I'll keep Emilia stirring while I cook the pasta." Elliott winked at her.

Cady dragged her into the hallway next to the kitchen.

"What is going on? Are you guys…like…a couple? Did you sleep with him?" Cady's voice rose with each sentence.

Sophia kissed the top of her head. "First of all, I don't think my love life is any of your business, missy. And second of all—"

"Yes it is! Emilia and I sent you on that mission. If something is going on, I want to know. And make sure…you know…you're safe."

Sophia choked. "Are you talking about birth control? Cady!"

"No! Don't be crazy. I'm talking about your heart, Mom. You barely know this guy. He's so temperamental. I don't want you to get hurt. You're still recovering."

Sophia cupped her daughter's face. "Sweetheart, I'm an adult. And to be honest with you, I feel better today than I have in months. Truly. This show has been good for me. Good for me to get out of the house, away from…memories. Learn to be a little bit independent. Try new things."

"You mean, like a Scottish guy?"

Sophia and Cady broke down into giggles.

"Hey! Don't leave me out of this conversation." Emilia

turned up, wiping her hands on an apron. "So spill. What's going on, Mom?"

Sophia looked at her girls, standing side-by-side, so beautiful, a mix of her and David and their very own spirits. She reached out and grabbed their hands, squeezing them in reassurance.

"I just want you both to know. I love you. And thank you. This competition has been good for me. I forgot that I can do things on my own. I forgot that I'm..." She took a deep breath. "I'm...me. Not just part of 'David and Sophia.' But Sophia. Alone. And that doesn't have to be a bad thing. It's the new thing. And I have to embrace this and make it good. For all of us."

The girls slid their arms around her and leaned against her shoulders. They sobbed quietly, and she just held them and let them cry. Let all of them cry for what was lost, what was new, what was coming.

Emilia wiped the tears from Sophia's cheek. "And the Beast? Elliott? Do you trust him?"

"Yes, I do. He is incredibly strong-willed, and sensitive, and authentic, and"—*and intense and passionate and exciting and*—"yes. I trust him."

"Mom, I think he needs you." Emilia summed things up as usual.

Sophia stared into her older daughter's eyes, dark and insightful and shocking in their spot-on assessment of people and places and things. "I think you're right."

"Ladies!" A shout from the kitchen had them all turning to the doorway. "Who's ready for lunch?"

"I'm ready," Sophia answered without hesitation.

And by God, it was the truth.

🥐 🥐 🥐

"So, Chef Adamson, what do you do when you're not

cooking?" Cady twirled strands of linguine around her spoon and dipped it into the creamy red sauce.

"I sleep."

"Seriously. You cook and sleep…that's it? I find that very difficult to believe."

"Believe it, Daughter Number Two."

Cady turned to Sophia. "Why does he keep calling me Daughter Number Two and chuckling?"

Sophia smiled. "Because he calls his ex-wives Wife Number One, Two, and Three. He's funny like that."

"You have *three* ex-wives?" Emilia whistled.

Elliott did not look amused. "Aye. It's true. I spent about ninety-five percent of my time on the restaurants and five percent on the marriages. Clearly, five percent is not enough. That was a mistake. My wives deserved better." He swallowed a sip of his red wine. "And ninety-five percent wasn't enough for the restaurants either. I'm not doing very well in either arena."

"You're such a good cook. Why aren't your restaurants doing well?" Cady asked.

"Because Elliott ignores his customers, the space, the ambience, and all the other details that go into running a restaurant. Except the food. Isn't that right, Beast?" Sophia wondered how

Elliott would respond to the cold, hard truth.

"Who told you that? Helene?" he barked.

"Who's Helene? One of his ex-wives?" Emilia whispered to her mother.

"No, Helene is an opinionated French busy-body," Elliott said. He scratched his beard in annoyance.

"Helene is an accomplished chef and a wise woman. And I think down deep inside of Elliott he knows she's right."

"Bah."

"I'm a design student. Did you know that, Elliott?" Cady smirked. "Guess what my final project was this semester? Designing a restaurant!"

"That's nice," he said with no inflection whatsoever.

"I've been managing a café on campus for the last year," Emilia added.

"God save me from opinionated and interfering women," Elliott whispered under his breath.

"If Elliott weren't such an ogre, he could pick your brilliant brains and perhaps come up with some new ideas for his failing restaurant," Sophia said.

His gaze snapped up. "I need money. That's all. Money."

"You need a lot more than money, Elliott. You need some new inspiration."

"I like cooking Scottish food, Sophia."

"I'm not talking about that. I'm talking about all the other stuff."

Elliott contemplated the ceiling and counted to ten. Em and Cady giggled the whole time.

"So, Elliott, you're *all* about Scottish food? Is that all you do?" Cady asked.

"*All?* Aye. Traditional preparation. I pay homage to the old ways, the true ways. I'm not into molecular gastronomy and other gimmicks." He crossed his arms belligerently.

"Don't you get bored with that?" Em asked. "I thought chefs liked trying new things."

Elliott rolled his eyes. "Bored? No. I respect Scottish tradition. I don't need to *elevate* the food or *update* the food. When I hear chefs talking about that it drives me insane." He spat out the words. "Why does Scottish cooking have to be elevated? Are the old ways not good enough? I respect years of tradition. That's my cooking approach, and it will be until the day I die."

Emilia opened her mouth to ask another question, but Elliott cut her off.

"Do you know that Cock-a-Leekie soup dates back to the sixteenth century? I remember butchering chickens with my mum and making the stock just the way she did with my nana.

With leeks and smoked bacon and fresh herbs bundled up—a bouquet garni. The old ways are the best ways."

Em sat quietly as Elliott took another sip of wine and glared at Sophia, daring her to argue with him.

"It's like the Christmas light thing. With Dad. When we tried to get him to switch to the little white lights," Cady said.

Em laughed. "Oh my God! I forgot about that."

Elliott frowned. "What lights?" he asked.

Cady continued, "We had these old Christmas tree lights. You know, the big ugly ones that are all the colors of the rainbow? The opposite of subtle and elegant. They were clunky and old-school."

"They belonged to Dad's parents, and we inherited them," Em said. "My father loved those things. They reminded him of his childhood."

Sophia smiled at Elliott. "And he *refused* to update the tree."

Cady nodded her head. "We had a huge family fight. Mom, Em, and I wanted to get the elegant little white lights and try something new. Dad was appalled. He refused."

"Stubborn. I like that," Elliott said. He smiled at Sophia and she smiled back.

"Oh yeah. Stubborn. Dad said those lights were good enough for two generations of Browns, and we didn't need the fancy ones. So that was the end of it. All of our friends had twinkly white lights on the tree, and we had the big fat clunkers." Emilia shook her head.

"And still do," Cady said.

Elliott stroked his beard. "I think I would have liked your father. He sounds like my kind of guy. Tell me more about him."

"What do you want to know?" Cady asked.

"How did he deal with three interfering busybodies?" Elliott asked straight-faced.

Emilia grinned. "We called him the Bumbling Professor.

171

He was always knee-deep in papers and work and assignments. He spent most of his time reading and writing."

Cady nodded. "It's true. He would be reading, and Mom would be dusting the table, and he would just lift the book at the exact second she needed him to. And then she'd dust under him. They were like a well-oiled machine."

Elliott poured himself more wine. "So he worked, and Sophia took care of the nest."

"Mom takes care of everyone," Emilia said.

"Yep. She took care of Dad, and us, of course. And the neighbors." Cady glanced at her mother.

"And her old friends from college."

"And the lady who checks us out at the general store." Cady giggled.

"And the baby birds that fall out of the trees into the garden." Emilia high-fived her sister.

Sophia laughed. "Enough. You guys are making me sound like Mother Teresa. I'm not that selfless. Please."

"I sort of think you are, Mom," Cady said. "You can't help yourself."

"Cady is right. You take care of everyone. Even me. You're worried about me, aren't you? My wives didn't even worry about me, Sophia. They couldn't have cared less if I went up in flames over the gas stove." Elliott reached for her hand.

"Maybe that's because you treated them like assistants, Elliott. You reap what you sow. You're lucky you didn't wake up one morning with a big machete sticking out of your back."

"I had to make a choice. My career. Or a family. The wives knew what I was like when they married me. They knew my first love was the kitchen."

"That sounds lonely," Cady said.

"I'm too busy fucking up my restaurants to be lonely," he grumbled. "Yes, well, evidently I'm reaping now. No wives, and a restaurant on the brink of collapse. If I don't win this contest, maybe I can get a job as Baldwin's sous-chef. What do you think, Sophia?"

"Never. You are the monarch of your kingdom, Beast. You just need to surround yourself with some talented friends. And treat them well."

Elliott smiled as he dug into his second plate of pasta. "Did I already say, 'save me from interfering women?'"

Chapter Eighteen

A ll right, ladies. Time for another cooking lesson. Your mother has informed me that all three of you have a 'wicked sweet tooth.' Is this true?" Elliott unwrapped the organic chocolate he'd purchased at the farmer's market.

"Aye!" Cady cheered. "Mom makes fabulous desserts. And Em and I are the happy recipients of her experiments."

Elliott stilled his hands and glanced at Sophia. "Your mother does make fabulous desserts. That's why I'm here right now."

Em frowned. "What do you mean?"

"Sorry, dearie, not allowed to discuss that. It's in the contract. On with the lesson. Today we're going to be making a delicious Scottish specialty—orange chocolate mousse. With whisky of course." He looked at the girls. "Are both of you old enough for whisky? Good," he said without waiting for an answer.

Cady giggled. "Yum. I love chocolate mousse."

"So do I," Em agreed. "What can we do to help?"

"I need four eggs separated, and an orange rind grated."

Sophia nudged his hip. "What about me?"

He nudged hers back. "I have a few ideas." He growled the words, low and soft in her ear.

Sophia felt a blush spread from her neck up the side of her face.

Elliott cleared his throat. "But if you're talking about the recipe, how about whisking some egg whites." He pushed his hip against her again.

All she could think about was heat. His massive body was like a furnace in the middle of her kitchen. He leaned down and nuzzled her lips, brushing his beard along the corner of her mouth.

"You taste like chocolate, Elliott." Sophia licked her lips and wished for one selfish moment that they were alone.

"You taste like forbidden fruit, sweet Sophia." He pressed his lips flush against her ear, so that only she could hear his words. "When do I get to taste you again? I can hardly wait." He bit out the words, soft but edged with desperation.

Sophia felt her soul fill with joy. Perhaps she was taming this beast after all.

"Ahem!" Cady swatted her mother on the butt with an old dishrag. "Let's not turn this into *that* kind of lesson. I thought we were making chocolate mousse?"

"Yeah," Emilia said. "There's no kissing in the Forget-Me-Not Café. That's an automatic disqualification."

Elliott reluctantly pulled his attention away from Sophia and faced the girls. "What's the Forget-Me-Not Café?"

"Mom's old dream. She thought about opening a bistro in town. I even painted a sign for her. But then Grandma got sick and dad became head of the history department, and she got too busy. Now we call her kitchen the Forget-Me-Not Café."

"Is that true, Sophia?" Elliott regarded her with a thoughtful expression.

"Dreams from long ago." She shrugged and refused to

look him in the eye. Afraid he would see too much this time. See that it wasn't such a toss-away dream, and that maybe the disappointment still stung.

"So you sacrificed a career for your family. And I sacrificed my family for a career."

She glanced up at him, shocked by the quiet intensity of his words.

Was it true? They stared at each other, her hands still clutching the whisk and his fingers gripping the whisky bottle, holding on for dear life. He held onto something comforting, something Scottish. And what was she holding onto?

Cady boosted herself onto the counter and peered out the window. "Hey! I have a good idea. The garden is packed with *Viola*. Let's make some candied violets for the dessert. That will look adorable on top of the chocolate mousse."

Sophia was thankful for Cady's interruption. She ripped her gaze away from Elliott and smiled at her youngest daughter. "Good idea, honey. Let's make Elliott play with flowers for a change." Her voice wobbled a bit.

Elliott set down the bottle of whisky and wrapped his arms around her from behind.

Maybe she hadn't hid the disappointment as well as she thought. She leaned back against his hard chest and sighed.

"You've raised a whole family of garden sprites, I see." He whispered the words into the top of her hair. "Do you put flowers on everything?"

Sophia smiled up at him. "Everything edible."

"We like to accessorize," Em said.

"Your food?" Elliott shook his head.

"Why not? We have tons of flowers in the garden, and they make Mom's desserts look gorgeous," Cady said.

Elliott rolled his eyes. "I think your daughter would like Jenny the Blogger. The two of them could accessorize all the platters for dinner."

"Hm. I'm not too sure about that," Sophia answered. "But I agree about the candied violets. Let's teach Elliott something today." She turned in his arms. "What do you think, Chef Adamson? Are you ready for a lesson?"

He barked out a laugh.

"I don't know about this," Em said. "Elliott seems a bit heavy-handed. He'll probably beat the shit out of those flowers."

Cady shook her head sadly. "Yep. Turn them into compost."

Emilia folded her arms across her chest. "I suppose we can try to teach him some cooking techniques. But we're going to need *a lot* of patience."

Elliott chuckled. "I can see you ladies won't be satisfied until I'm dancing in the garden with you. Fine. You can teach me how to make candied violets, and I'll get you all drunk on good Scottish whisky."

And so they did. The three Brown women showed Elliott how to pluck the flower heads off *Viola tricolor* and line them up on a sheet of parchment. They painted them with egg whites and water and giggled as Elliott sprinkled sugar on the blossoms. He sang a naughty Scottish ditty while he worked, and Em and Cady made up some new lyrics that had him roaring with laughter.

And when the mousse was done, flavored with orange and whisky and topped with violets, the four of them toasted their success by devouring the desserts, flowers and all. They stood in the kitchen and licked the bottom of their bowls. The afternoon sun slanted in through the windows and turned Elliott's dark blue eyes into the color of sea glass. Eyes that followed Sophia as she moved about the kitchen, cleaning pots and putting away the dishes. Eyes filled with promises, dark and deep and delicious.

And even though Sophia knew they hadn't imbibed enough whisky to get tipsy, she felt a little bit drunk.

In a good way.

❦ ❦ ❦

"And this one?" Elliott pointed to a photo on the mantel. "Where was this taken?"

"That was taken in Bermuda. On my honeymoon. I was twenty-four."

"David looks smitten with you. Look at him, ignoring the turquoise sea, eyes only for you."

"Hmm. For a few minutes, maybe. Until the latest issue of *Medieval History* arrived in the mailbox."

Elliott chuckled. "It's hard to compete with decapitations and blood-thirsty monarchs."

"Yes, it is." Sophia lifted another frame. "This is one of my favorites. The girls in their little rowboat on the Cape. They were looking for mermaids."

"An admirable mission." Elliott slid an arm around her waist.

The girls were out with friends, having a beer at the local pub. So she and Elliott were alone. It was odd to be alone with a man other than David in this house. And one with such a huge presence, big and bold. And sexy. She kept seeing his head between her legs, bobbing as he feasted. With so much enthusiasm and noise. She wanted that again. She wanted it tonight.

Elliott squeezed her hip. "I was nervous about coming here. I thought I would feel uncomfortable in your late husband's home. Like an interloper. But this house feels like *your* house. I don't sense him that much."

"I guess you're right. It's always been a woman's home, with the three of us. David would usually steal away to his office at the college. Or curl up in the corner and read."

She pointed to the recliner. "That was his usual spot. The reading nook. With his chair and his little side table. And the lamp that illuminated his bald spot."

Elliott rubbed his bare head. "That might be the only thing the two of us have in common."

"In some ways, we were leading parallel lives. I did my thing, and he did his thing. But his quiet presence was always comforting to me. It was always there, making me feel safe. And when it was gone…"

"What happened?" Elliott kissed her forehead.

Maybe the distraction of Sophia's life was good for him. It temporarily dismissed the anxiety of tomorrow's final.

"What happened? We were all just plugging along. You probably think this life—my old life—was boring as hell. Gardening, cooking, visiting with the girls."

"I think it sounds lovely. You held your family together all those years. And you're still doing it. Don't downplay your strength, Sophia."

"I did my best, I suppose. But when David had his heart attack, it was like a bomb exploded in our lives. It left a huge gaping hole in our family, one that I couldn't fix. Couldn't possibly fix. It was too big, too destructive. We were all lost. I was lost."

Elliott pulled her close to him and stroked her cheek. "You lost your old life." ·

She nodded. "I did."

"Time to make a new life."

She leaned against his chest and sighed. "Easier said than done. I'm too old to make a new life."

"Bullshit," he answered. "My Uncle Rory is eighty-two years old. He lost his wife after forty years of marriage. And now he's found a widow from our town, and they walk around holding hands like a couple of kids. You're not too old, Sophia. You can do it."

"I feel old. Although I must admit this past week has been good for me. Getting man-handled by a giant Scottish chef has been good for my spirits." She smiled at him.

Elliott laughed. "Uh-huh. Is that why you signed up for *A Taste of Heaven*? To pick up your spirits?"

"That's why the girls signed me up."

"But you didn't have to go. And you did go. That took courage."

"*You're* the courageous one, Elliott."

He shook his head. "No, you're wrong about that. I'm a stubborn bastard, but when the going gets tough, I would rather start fresh than try to fix things. It's the easy way out. The hard way is your way. Forced to fix the shambles left behind with the gaping hole. You're the one who is fearless, love. I'm just desperate."

"Maybe we both have courage, Elliott. And we forgot. I forgot I had it. And I think you forgot, too. But you're doing new things for the first time in fifty years. Cooking for children. Working with a partner. Maybe all those things you fear aren't so bad after all. What do you think?"

He leaned down and kissed her, slowly, seductively, wet and hot and naughty. "I think I want to go to bed."

They went to bed.

"I've been waiting for this all day." Sophia unbuttoned his shirt with shaky fingers. She felt giddy with anticipation.

"So have I. You're driving me crazy. You know I have an embarrassing crush on you, Mrs. Brown." He leaned down and nuzzled her neck.

A thrill shot through her. "You do? Ordinary Mrs. Brown?"

"There is nothing ordinary about you, love." He pulled off her blouse and flung it onto the floor. "Ah…so sweet." He cupped her breasts through the lacy bra.

She whimpered with pleasure.

"How long will the girls be gone?" he asked.

She shook her head in a daze. His big rough hands had already pushed down the cups of her bra and were fondling her breasts. "I-I don't know. A few hours."

Elliott lifted her in his arms and dropped her onto the bed. "Thank God. I want to be able to make some noise for a change. And hear you make noise. Fucking in the dorm with the creaky bed and unwanted neighbors was a big pain in the ass."

He stared down at her, lying boneless on the bed, and his nostrils flared. "Jesus H. Christ, you are sexy. And deceiving, too."

She propped herself up on her elbows. "Deceiving? How so?"

He crawled onto the bed on all fours and hovered above her. She could smell his scent—strong and wicked. She wanted that fragrance all over her body.

"You look like a sweet little garden sprite, but underneath you are fierce as hell. Strong-willed. A true competitor. Who knew?" Elliott kissed her softly. Small little kisses, along the seams of her lips. Brushing his beard on her chin.

She slid her arms around his neck and pulled him down for another kiss. This one not so gentle. He growled and Sophia smiled.

"I didn't know. Not until this week."

"I've never met anyone like you. You are a force to be reckoned with. And you really have no idea. You think you're ordinary, but you're not."

She arched against him. She was feeling impatient, and his pants were still on. "I have no idea what you're talking about, Chef Adamson. But how about losing those pants?"

He rolled off the bed and unbuttoned his jeans. "You have no idea? You won the first challenge on a high level cooking competition. And you're an amateur! Because you were willing to take an insane risk with that dessert. Your experience and confidence as a mother won us that goddamned cheese contest. You butchered a turkey for the first time while Herman puked his guts out. And you've managed to deal with me—my temper, my insecurities, everything—day after day. My ex-wives couldn't do it. My mentors couldn't do it. You've done it. Don't tell me you're ordinary." He stripped off his pants.

She reached for his erection.

Elliott laughed. "See? You're bossy. And delicious to boot."

The Scottish giant had a crush on her! And she did feel fierce in his presence. And powerful. Perhaps some part of her was indeed fierce, and it was bubbling up through the cracks.

"Give it a good, hard yank, love." He stared at her tiny hand on his cock. "Don't be shy. Be greedy tonight. Take and take and take. It's about time you learned to be selfish. It's not such a bad thing, is it?"

She gazed at him, at his nude body covered with reddish-gold hair, thick and manly and aroused. Could she take? Selfishly? It turned her on, the thought of that. It was so unlike her, the sweet little doll with the big brown eyes. She'd been waiting all day as the sexual tension coiled up inside of her. She was tired of being good.

"Let's see you get a little bit wild, sweetheart." Elliott cracked a wicked smile and reached for her panties. He slid them off her legs and tossed them aside.

She crooked a finger at the giant, inviting him to join her. "Let's go, Chef. You want wild? I'll give you wild."

As soon as he kneeled on the bed, Sophia pushed him onto his back and straddled him. He laughed and steadied her with his thick arms.

"I like it already." He raised a brow, taunting her. "What's next?" His breathing was labored, and his cock bobbed in front of her enticingly.

She flipped her hair over and let it trail along his body, teasing him with a feather-light touch. And then she leaned down and used her mouth, nipping, licking, and sucking the earthy taste of Elliott Adamson. He bucked with enthusiasm.

"Harder, sweetheart. Yes. Christ, that's it."

For the first time in twenty-four years, there was another man in her bed. David had been whipcord thin and muscular. With the body of a long-distance runner, and his mind set on the end line. This man in her bed was different. Powerful, heavy, loud, and brash. Short-tempered. Fearless. It was a heady sensation, having this beast beneath her, at her beck and call. Gazing at her with rapture.

She worked her way back up his belly and chest, nipping along the way, sucking hard on his nipples. He released a half laugh, half groan and slid his hands around to squeeze her bottom as she straddled him again.

"What do you want, Sophia? Tell me."

And that was the real question, wasn't it? What did she really want?

She avoided answering by sinking down on his erection, all the way down. Until she felt the softness of his sac sliding along her bottom. She rode him that way, and his eyes were glued to her breasts, which swayed with each stroke. He was covered with sweat. She'd done that. Made the Beast sweat and groan. She liked who she was with Elliott. Daring enough to be wild and greedy.

He reached up to pinch her nipples. "You're enjoying this, aren't you? Torturing me." He choked out a laugh. "We really do look like Beauty and the Beast."

"We do?" She could barely form a response.

"Aye. I'm hairy and rough, and you're like a woodland fairy. All you need is a crown of flowers in your dark hair, and I swear, I can see you floating through the forest."

"Teasing you?" She splayed her fingers on his slick chest.

"Aye. That's for goddamned sure. But I've caught you now, sweetheart. Haven't I? At least for this moment, you belong to me."

He flipped her, and she loved it. The feeling of his weight pushing her down into the mattress. He gazed at her with desire and something else. Something intense and needy. Some part of the Beast was vulnerable, and that look shook her to the core.

Every time he entered her was an event. Into her mouth, between her legs, he entered slowly, making sure she was aware of the invasion. That she welcomed him, acknowledged him.

And then he would go so deep, she thought she would lose her mind. He was every bit as wild as she, and they spurred each other on. He laughed each time, thrilled to make the good little widow thrash in wild abandon.

They rolled around on her bed all night. Tangled together on the knotted sheets, listening to the sound of crickets and frogs, and eventually the songbirds, outside her window. Elliott finally fell asleep, just as the sun rose over her neighbor's barn in a spectacular show of magenta and apricot. Sophia sighed and snuggled into his embrace, feeling peaceful and content. She liked this new Sophia. The one who was bold and unafraid. It was time to let the old one go.

Chapter Nineteen

Welcome back to *A Taste of Heaven*!" Mr. Smith cheered and waved the freshly ironed flag over his head. "It's the big day—the final challenge for our two last pairs. Sophia Brown, the amateur from Vermont, and Elliott Adamson, professional chef and owner of Stone Soup in North Berwick, Scotland, are in one corner."

As the camera panned over their faces, Sophia forced herself to smile. Elliott didn't even bother. He looked ready to throttle someone. As usual.

"And in the other corner, we have amateur cook Kevin Holt from North Carolina, paired with Chef Michael Baldwin, owner of three award-winning restaurants in Chicago. Welcome to our final contest!"

The judges and eliminated contestants were seated to the side of the courtyard garden. They clapped and cheered, and Sophia heard a few nicknames hollered, including *Beauty and the Beast*. That was a good sign.

"We've spent the week exploring Vermont and its

products—a creamery, a turkey farm. We've cooked with organic beef and locally-grown fruits and vegetables. We've had the ultimate farm-to-table experience. And now for our final challenge, we'll be showcasing another famous Vermont staple. Probably the most popular and quintessential Vermont product—maple syrup." Mr. Smith lifted a glass vial filled with amber liquid. "Our final two pairs will prepare a meal that highlights maple syrup that has been collected right here on the Vermont Culinary Institute campus. I'm sure you all have noticed the beautiful sugar maples surrounding us."

Elliott started to tap his foot. Sophia touched his arm gently, and he stopped.

"But we have a few surprises for you today, as well." Mr. Smith rubbed his hands together.

Both Elliott and Michael said *"fuck"* at the same time.

"Our final pairs will need some extra hands. So we brought some helpers along. In keeping with our amateur concept, these assistants are not professionally trained. But they more than make up for that with their enthusiasm. Their loyalty. And their love." Mr. Smith gestured to the kitchen door and a small group of people appeared.

When Sophia saw Cady and Emilia she covered her mouth with her hand.

There were three groups of people. Em and Cady. A group of young adults waving at Kevin. And Sophia saw a young woman and an older gentleman saluting Chef Baldwin. When she turned to Elliott, her heart sank. His face was white. Where was Elliott's family? He had only mentioned his elderly Uncle Rory. Perhaps he was too old to travel.

She reached over to take Elliott's hand, but he was stiff as stone. His fingers refused to yield.

Her heart broke for him.

Mr. Smith gestured to the eliminated amateurs and invited them to join the group. "As you can see, we've found some very willing assistants for you today. Sophia's daughters are here. Kevin's three sons are with us today from North

Carolina. And Chef Baldwin's sister and father have joined us, too." He turned to Elliott and shrugged. "Unfortunately, Elliott's uncle was unable to manage the flight all the way from Scotland, so you'll have the option of choosing one of the eliminated amateurs as an assistant today."

Elliott barely nodded a response.

"Sophia, you're up first. You get to pick one of your daughters as an assistant."

Cady yelled, "Pick me, pick me!" She waved her arms over her head.

Sophia laughed through her tears.

Emilia pointed to Cady behind her back and mouthed *"Pick her"* to her mother.

"I guess I'll choose my younger daughter Cady today. She seems ready for the challenge," Sophia said. Cady rushed to her and threw herself into Sophia's arms.

"Surprise! We knew about this yesterday, but we managed to keep it a secret. How about that?" Cady bit her lip impishly.

"Sneaky girl," Sophia whispered to her daughter.

"Chef Baldwin, who is your choice?" Mr. Smith had both Michael and Kevin choose their assistants, and then he turned to Elliott.

"And Elliott, since your uncle couldn't join us today, which one of the amateurs would you like to include on your team for the final?"

Elliott's face was completely devoid of emotion. As Kevin and his son linked arms and Chef Baldwin and his sister whispered together, Elliott inspected the remaining chefs. He was all alone. Sophia thought about the photos she'd seen of him standing in front of the stone wall in North Berwick. With the wind rippling his clothes and a gray sky framing his solitary figure. She felt sick inside. This wasn't right.

She looked over the group of amateurs. Tammy, Nathan, Herman, and the others. None of them would be able to deal with Elliott and his temper. She made eye contact with Emilia, and Sophia knew they were both thinking the same thing.

"Mr. Smith, I have an idea." Sophia's voice cracked with tension.

The producer looked startled. "What can I help you with, Sophia?"

"Since Elliott is choosing an amateur, maybe you could throw my daughter Emilia into the mix. She's an amateur too."

Mr. Smith nodded slowly. "That's true. Emilia, would you be agreeable to that?"

Emilia regarded Elliott and answered, "Work with the Beast? I think so."

The audience laughed, and Sophia was relieved to hear a chuckle from Elliott.

"You know I'm not very nice to my assistants. Just ask your mum." Elliott folded his arms across his chest in an exaggerated motion.

"I can take it," Em replied. She crossed her arms, too.

"I don't like cooks with a heavy hand who beat the hell out of their tomatoes."

Emilia answered, "Good thing I don't do that...anymore."

Mr. Smith looked completely thrilled with this turn of events. Sophia could tell the banter between Emilia and Elliott would make for very good television. Thank God. She wanted Elliott to have someone on his side, really on his side. Not a poor loser who would throw him under the bus at the first opportunity.

Elliott turned to Mr. Smith and nodded. "I'll take Daughter Number One, Emilia. If I have to deal with another amateur assistant, it might as well be her."

Mr. Smith clapped his hands. "The two Brown girls are in the mix! I love it. Emilia, please join Chef Adamson."

Em first walked over to Sophia and hugged her. She fist-bumped her sister. And then she sashayed right up to Elliott and stood in front of him. "Hey, Beast. Need any tomatoes crushed today?"

Elliott looked down at her and lifted a brow. "No, but we have to figure out something fancy to do with maple syrup.

I'll be keeping you busy this afternoon."

She moved to his side. Elliott glanced over her head and caught Sophia's eye. The color had returned to his face. He nodded at her, almost imperceptibly. She knew what that nod meant and what it cost him. The Scottish giant, full of pride and bluster, was sending her a nod of gratitude. Sophia smiled to herself. He'd unintentionally become ensnared by a trio of woodland sprites. Probably against his will. But what was done was done.

Mr. Smith motioned for the others to sit. "Remember when I told you on the first day that your *amuse-bouche* challenge would be the *only* time you cooked alone? Well, I lied." He raised an eyebrow. "This final challenge has two parts. One, the pair must prepare a delicious meal and dessert with the highlighted food. And two, each of the finalists must prepare one dish…*alone*. It may or may not include maple syrup, but it must reflect your personal style and approach to cooking. Your assistant may help but your partner can't be part of this challenge. The judges will be looking at all the final dishes when we make our decision."

Elliott grumbled under his breath. Sophia knew he didn't like surprises. All in all, he was holding up pretty well.

As Mr. Smith continued describing the rules for the last challenge, Sophia noticed that Emilia had slipped her hand into Elliott's. Cady noticed too. And then her younger daughter linked their hands, and Sophia felt the threads of her family weaving them together, and for a moment on this sunny August day, all felt right with the world.

◊ ◊ ◊

"Salmon. We do salmon." Elliott scribbled on his notebook as Em peered over his shoulder.

The four of them were huddled around their worktable discussing their options.

"Salmon with a whisky-maple glaze. I'll use Laphroaig."

Elliott looked up. "Sophia, what do you think? We will be able to get a nice piece of fish?"

She nodded. "Yes, the salmon should be excellent."

"Mom, what are you going to cook for your part of the dish?" Cady perched on the edge of the table.

"I have an idea. That will combine some Scottish favorites with some other flavors."

"Uh-oh. I don't know if I like the sound of that." Elliott groaned.

"Give her a chance, Beast," Em said.

Sophia laughed. "Three girls against the Beast. The poor man doesn't stand a chance."

He rolled his eyes. "Get on with it, woman. What's your idea?"

"Salmon with whisky-maple glaze, surrounded by a trio of colors—peas with mint, carrots with maple and thyme, and neeps and tatties with nutmeg and parsley. Green, orange, white. And we can put the salmon on a bed of risotto and mushrooms."

Elliott frowned. He tapped his pencil on the table. "I love the trio of colors. And the fact that you're incorporating more Scottish dishes. But I don't do risotto."

"I do." Emilia raised her hand. "I love making risotto. I have the patience to do it."

Sophia slid an arm around her oldest daughter's shoulders. "She does. And she's great at it."

Elliott released a slow hiss. The entire contest was on the line, and he was relinquishing control. During the most important meal of his life. Sophia watched his gaze dart back and forth among the three women. He finally closed his eyes and nodded.

"Very well, don't fuck up."

Emilia and Cady laughed.

"What about me? I'm good at desserts," Cady grabbed the pencil from Elliott. "How about this?" She scribbled a little drawing on his notebook.

He smiled. "Hmm. I like it, Cady. I like it a lot."

"Show us," Emilia demanded.

Elliott turned the page so they could all see. Cady had drawn a goblet filled with layers of peaches and brown sugar and rum and shortbread crumbs, topped with maple whipped cream.

"I love the Scottish shortbread in here. Let's add a cookie to the top." Elliott drew that onto the picture.

"I'll make some candied violets for a garnish. It will look spectacular. And since Elliott has now been trained, he can be my sous-chef." Cady smirked.

Elliott chuckled and patted Cady on the head. "Nice try. I approve of the candied violets, especially since Jenny will adore that idea." He added some more notations onto the menu. "And let's cut the richness of this meal with a little palate cleanser between the entrée and dessert. How about tipsy oranges?"

"Oh. That sounds good. How do you make that?" Sophia leaned closer to him, needing to feel his heat. He pressed his arm against hers, instinctively reacting to her needs. How had this happened so fast? This connection between them?

"Easiest thing in the world. Section the orange, drizzle Drambuie on top, sprinkle some brown sugar on there and broil quickly to get the sugar bubbling. Add some fresh mint. A quick, refreshing stop before Cady's decadent dessert." He glanced at Sophia. "What say you, Beauty? Do I get your seal of approval?"

"Aye, Beast, you do." She ignored Cady and Emilia's snickers. "I think we better get to work. We have a lot to do."

He nodded at her again. His relaxed expression made Sophia feel settled and self-assured. She had finally earned his trust.

Elliott ripped off a couple of pages from his notebook and handed them to the girls. "Here are the lists. We knock things off one at a time. If there are any problems, check with me right away. Don't try to *wing* it. I don't like winging it."

"What about your individual courses?" Cady asked.

"Em and I will work on that on our own. And you and Sophia will do the same."

Emilia put her fist in the middle of their huddle. "Game time. Let's do this."

Cady added her fist on top, and then Sophia. And finally Elliott with an off-center smile. "Let's Go Team Grumpy Scottish Bastard."

"And Team Beauty and the Beast," Sophia added.

"Beauties. I'm surrounded by three beauties." Elliott clucked. "I just hope you three beauties know how to cook. Let's go."

Chapter Twenty

If there had ever been a surreal moment in Sophia's life, this was it. With an audience watching her every move, cameras in her face, Mr. Smith bobbing around the set with exaggerated enthusiasm, and a flawless blue sky overhead. It was difficult to reconcile the peacefulness of a perfect August day in Vermont with the anxiety of this television show. She was worried for Elliott, anxious for her daughters, and nervous about her own performance.

As she prepared her meal, she sneaked glances at Elliott and Emilia. At first Elliott was strictly business, chopping and fussing and barking orders. But Emilia dished it right back. She teased and mocked, and eventually Sophia was shocked to see Elliott smile. She couldn't remember ever seeing him smile while he cooked during the show. But he and Emilia were working out some sort of partnership.

Cady ran to the garden and gathered fresh thyme and mint. She grated the nutmeg, chopped the parsley, all the while chattering and laughing and reminding Sophia that this moment was just part of the whole. In the grand scheme of things, not as important as other moments. Surprisingly, Sophia began to enjoy the cooking. Knowing that Cady was with her and Emilia had Elliott's back took away a huge chunk of anxiety.

Her sweet little girls, searching for mermaids and seashells, were all grown up. They'd turned into thoughtful, kind adults with insights about life and living that made Sophia proud to be their parent.

"So, Sophia, how is it working out with you and Cady?" Mr. Smith leaned over their worktable. "Everything looks delicious."

"We're doing very well, thank you. Cady is an enthusiastic cook."

"And how about Elliott and Emilia? Can she handle the Beast? That's a tall order."

Elliott was stirring the maple glaze on the stovetop and instructing Em about the consistency. Sophia thought they were adorable. Evidently, so did Mr. Smith. He had the camera crew hustle over to their table.

"Emilia, is the Beast giving you some cooking pointers?" Mr. Smith asked.

Emilia nodded. "Uh-huh. I just wanted to pour the whole bottle of whisky in there, but Elliott said we had to save some for later. For drinking, of course."

Sophia bit her lip to keep from laughing, but Cady burst out giggling.

Mr. Smith didn't know what to do. Elliott saved him the trouble.

"Naughty. I'll take that." Elliott removed the whisky bottle from Emilia's hands and put it back under the table. He looked at Sophia and raised an eyebrow.

Sophia smiled back. Emilia had managed to get Elliott relaxed for the final challenge. God bless her wonderful daughter.

The remaining hours flew by. After finishing their main course and dessert, she and Cady prepared her extra dish. Sophia had decided to make the girls' favorite dinner—beef tenderloin with peppercorn sauce. Soon enough they were plating and rushing back and forth to the huge banquet table set up in the courtyard. Pouring wine and adjusting garnishes and offering smiles to the judges.

The ambience of this meal was Sophia's idea of romance. The table was draped with ivory linen and topped with glass jars of flowers. Bouquets of *Rosa rugosa* and Queen Anne's lace were nestled among votives and bottles of wine. The local glassblower had provided an assortment of pottery dishes and hand-blown goblets. Strands of white lights dangled from the surrounding trees.

She and Elliott and the girls plated together, having reached some sort of exhausted Zen state. Emilia scooped the risotto, Elliott placed the salmon on top, Sophia added the three tiny sides shaped with a round cookie cutter. Elliott drizzled his sauce onto the final product. He brushed his shoulder against Sophia each time, needing that physical connection. The plates looked exquisite, artistic. Perfect.

She tried to ignore the overwhelming stress of the moment and focus on the food. Cady and Emilia added garnishes—fresh herbs and flowers. And Cady had a whole sheet of candied violets ready to sprinkle on their dessert. It made Elliott laugh and tease them all about being a family of garden sprites. When they finally got to the head of the table and faced a sea of critics, Sophia felt confident about their choices. They'd prepared a beautiful meal that successfully showcased Elliott's love for Scottish tradition, local Vermont products, and the Brown family's love of fresh vegetables and herbs. All the components had meshed together into one cohesive meal.

She still did not know the identity of Elliott's "secret" bonus dish. That was hidden from sight.

Chef Baldwin and Kevin also seemed pleased with their

results. Sophia sent Kevin a reassuring smile, and he nodded at her. Michael caught her eye with a death stare. Evidently she was no longer on his "friend" list.

Mr. Smith stood at the head of the table and lifted his wine glass. "To all of our judges, guests, and critics this evening... welcome! What a feast our contestants have prepared for us. I am truly touched and impressed by the talent I'm seeing tonight. And I think we can all agree that having this gorgeous Vermont setting as a backdrop for our finale is the icing on the heavenly cake."

Elliott reached over and squeezed Sophia's hand. "Save me from another bad food pun, please."

Sophia laughed. She reached for Cady's hand, and soon she and her daughters and Elliott were all linked, hand-in-hand, awaiting the final judgment. She turned to look at Elliott, to see how he was doing, and she was surprised to find him leaning down and laughing at a comment from Cady. His bright white teeth flashed from that luscious beard, and then his gaze found hers. And at that moment, Sophia realized winning the contest had ceased to be the all-consuming goal. This was the moment she'd been working towards.

A moment of happiness, pure and simple.

Her senses were no longer muted. The sky was as blue as a field of lupine, the fragrance of rugosa roses filled the air, the rough touch of Elliott's fingers made her heart flutter and race, the taste of maple was sweet on her tongue. All of these things, these simple things that had washed away from her life had come back. Did she still want to win?

She wanted to win for Elliott. Because he needed it. But for her, it was no longer necessary. Was it possible that this surreal experience was binding together the edges of the gaping hole of her life? Perhaps it was.

"Judges, what are your thoughts about tonight's dinner?" Mr. Smith sat down at the head of the table as the judges commenced their critique.

"What a wonderful way to celebrate maple syrup and Vermont!" Chef Rutgers stood and faced the contestants. "Maple pairs beautifully with salmon—which was cooked perfectly by the way, Chef Adamson—and is a favorite Scottish dish. I love that you combined the Vermont product with your Scottish traditions. And Chefs Baldwin and Holt used their maple syrup to create an inspired barbecue marinade for their sirloin steaks. Another winner."

Tarquin also stood. "I agree with Jonathan. Both of the entrees were splendid. I adored the sides contributed by Sophia and her daughter—the trio of colors and textures and tastes. Also with a nod to Scottish cooking, but clearly utilizing the fresh vegetables from our own courtyard garden. Very, very nice, Sophia." Chef Bailey saluted them.

Cady hugged Sophia and squealed with happiness.

Jenny walked over to the contestants and offered everyone a kiss on the cheek. She was clearly attempting a "warm, homey" feeling as the amateur representative. The chefs tolerated the gesture, but Sophia could tell that everyone was anxious to get on with the judging.

Jenny patted her stomach. "What a meal! I loved both of the entrees and all of the sides. Including the contrast of the spicy slaw and corn with Chef Baldwin's meal. As a southern gal, I can totally get behind that kind of heat." She winked.

Michael and Kevin high-fived each other.

"But I have to admit that the real star of the show for me was dessert. Although the maple ice cream from Team Baldwin and Holt was creamy and decadent, the peach-shortbread trifle from Team Beauty and the Beast was an absolute show-stopper. With the rum and the maple whipped cream and the precious candied violets. Oh my Lord! I could not get enough of that."

Elliott released a half laugh-half sob and turned to hug Cady. He lifted her into the air and she squeaked out loud.

"Beast! Put me down!"

Sophia and Em laughed.

Elliott slipped his arm around Sophia's daughters. "Beautiful and they can cook. Thank the good God."

"I have to agree about dessert. Chef Adamson's dish came out on top this time," Jonathan said.

"But we haven't discussed the individual courses," Tarquin added, looking amused. "This contest just keeps getting better and more entertaining."

Jenny shook her head. "If you say so."

Uh-oh. What now? Sophia glanced at Elliott. He had a determined expression on his face. And stubborn. That look made her nervous.

Jonathan lifted a napkin covering the individual plates for Team Baldwin and Holt. They had prepared two more beef dishes. Sophia bit her lip. She hoped her tenderloin would be able to stack up against these.

"Two lovely beef contributions from our all-male team," he said. And then he lifted the other napkin.

He didn't.

He did.

Sophia saw her delicate slices of tenderloin, nestled in a sauce with multi-colored peppercorns, right next to a plate with a plump piece of haggis.

He did.

The stomach was split open on the plate, exposing the haggis inside.

"Chef Adamson used a mixture of beef, lamb, and pancetta for his haggis. And of course the sheep stomach for presentation." Jonathan let out a hearty chuckle. "God bless you, Adamson. I didn't think you'd go for it, but you did. And I have to say this was absolutely delicious. The best haggis I've ever tasted."

Tarquin approached Elliott and shook his hand. "Delicious twist on haggis. Well-played."

Jenny smiled at the final four contestants. "I loved all of

the beef dishes, especially Michael's meatballs and Sophia's wonderful tenderloin." She glared at Elliott. "However, I was not as impressed with the haggis as my fellow judges. I'm all about *dressing up your dinner*, remember? And haggis is just not attractive. It's not tasty, in my humble opinion, and it certainly isn't nice to look at. Dear Lord." Jenny grimaced for the camera and the audience laughed.

Sophia was afraid to look at Elliott, but when she finally glanced his way, she was surprised to see a look of triumph on his face. This was his moment. The quintessential Scottish dish, laid open on the plate for their entire television audience. And at least two of the judges loved it.

It was a bold move. A courageous move. An utterly fearless choice.

Mr. Smith turned to Emilia. "Just curious. What did you think about this Scottish delicacy?"

"I loved it. It tastes like liver. My mom used to make us liverwurst and cream cheese sandwiches when we were little. It was nostalgic for me. And Elliott is so proud of his heritage, it was wonderful to see him prepare this traditional Scottish dish. Anyone can make meatballs."

Chef Baldwin glared at Emilia, but Elliott's expression stopped him cold. Sophia knew right at that moment that he would do anything to protect her daughters, and she felt the threads tighten a little bit more on her wounds. Was it possible that she was finally healing?

Harold Smith walked to the front of the table like a monarch overlooking his kingdom. With its silly little flags and scurrying cameramen to capture every moment, every disappointment, and the thrill of victory. "Finally, the decision we've been working towards all week. Which pair came out on top tonight? Judges? What say you?"

Tarquin, Jonathan, and Jenny joined their producer in front of the audience. It was a tense moment, but Sophia could only focus on one thing. Elliott. He was still as stone and barely breathing. She squeezed his hand, and he turned to look at her, releasing a long, slow breath.

"Thank you, Sophia."

"Thank *you*, Elliott."

"Hey. What about me? What am I? Chopped liver?" Emilia fake punched Elliott in the side.

He chuckled. "You did fine, Daughter Number One. Just fine. And you, too, Cady. Beautiful dessert, sweetheart."

Both of the girls smiled. They were sparkling for the cameras with their tousled black curls and dark eyes and spattering of freckles. Sophia's daughters captured that lovely feeling somewhere between the innocence and exuberance of youth and the adult-like comprehension of the gravity of this moment.

"One of these pairs found the magic. That magic in the kitchen when two different points of view mesh into one perfect meal." Tarquin's bow tie was bright orange tonight.

Jonathan clasped his hands behind his back. "And one of these meals managed to showcase rich cultural traditions with fresh ingredients and creativity."

Sophia was sure that Elliott had stopped breathing altogether. She was afraid he would turn blue and fall over on the table. She inched closer to him.

"For me, this partnership took everything to the next level with beautiful presentation and color and whimsy. Not only was the meal well-dressed, but ultimately, it was delicious, too. Which is obviously the most important part of our dinner. Right?" Jenny winked at the camera.

Sophia wondered what she had up her sleeve. She seemed way too perky.

Mr. Smith placed the flag on the table beside him. "I'm pleased to announce our favorite pair this evening." He shot the finalists a last, knowing smile. "Congratulations to Elliott and Sophia, who managed to combine Scottish and American flavors into a stunning meal."

For one moment, the silence was deafening. And then all hell broke loose. Cady jumped into the air and screamed. Emilia threw her arms around Elliott's neck and began to cry. The audience cheered and waved their blue and white flags, chanting and clapping as a fuming Chef Baldwin and his partner stepped back.

"Mom! Oh my God!" Cady grabbed her mother. "I told you! I told you! I knew you could do it."

The girls and Sophia laughed hysterically, and finally Sophia touched Elliott's arm.

He nodded once at her. His eyes were bright, searching hers. "Thank you. All of you." He took all three Brown girls and pulled them close.

Cady and Emilia giggled.

"Haggis? Really? What were you thinking?" Sophia managed to croak out the words in spite of her tears.

"My darling, sweet Sophia. You are my best luck charm, aren't you?" Elliott cupped her face with his giant hands and laughed. "My God, we did it. We actually fucking did it." He kissed her on the lips in front of all the cast and crew and judges and family members, and Sophia forgot to breathe.

"Just a minute. We're not done." Mr. Smith shouted above the noise. Everyone stopped and turned to see what he was talking about.

"I still have this check, remember?" He held an oversized check for fifty thousand dollars over his head. "But we have one last twist on this game. One last big announcement." He waggled his eyebrows.

A sick feeling of dread crept into Sophia's stomach. This was no time for twists. This was a time for celebration and relief.

Elliott stilled next to her. "What the fuck are they doing?"

Sophia didn't answer, but the smile that Jenny sent her made her skin break out in goosebumps.

Mr. Smith continued, "We wanted to see how our chefs,

both professional and amateur, would respond to being forced together into pairs for the challenges. If they could adjust, work together, and find a happy place for their creativity to blend and showcase the farm-to-table concept." He wiped his forehead with his ubiquitous linen hankie. "Some pairs worked, some didn't. But ultimately, we were still able to see the individual talents on the plate."

Elliott's grip was crushing her fingers.

"Sophia and Elliott were an impressive pair. But the producers of *A Taste of Heaven* knew, all along, that only one chef would win this competition."

Sophia's stomach dropped.

"Based on all the dishes prepared this week, including today's meal and individual courses, the judges have chosen one winner."

She looked up at Elliott's face. He stared down at her, with a small resigned smile. "Tricky bastards, are they not?"

"Elliott." She whispered his name.

Mr. Smith lifted the check over his head. "And the grand winner for *A Taste of Heaven* is Sophia Brown!"

"No," she whispered. "Elliott." Her body trembled in shock, but there was no sense of euphoria. Only a horrible sense of wrongness. The wrong man won. This was Elliott's day, not hers.

And then his strong arms were around her, embracing her, comforting her. "You won, Sprite. Smile for the camera."

"No. No. I can't—"

"Smile for the camera, love. It's all right." Elliott's eyes were shining.

"But Elliott. This is wrong. You know it is." Her voice was ragged.

"Sophia, smile for the camera. Play this game to its conclusion." Elliott gently pushed her forward toward the camera and the producers. Toward the judges who were hugging her and congratulating her. Toward the other contestants.

He didn't say a word. He didn't make a fuss. He didn't argue with the judges or question Sophia's win. The man from the first day of the contest would have yelled and screamed and forced a confrontation. But now he just stepped aside and let Sophia bask in her victory. He stepped aside for her.

The other chefs slapped Elliott on the back and teased him about the haggis. He grinned and chatted with them. All the while his eyes were locked onto Sophia, watching over her.

"Congratulations, Sophia!" Jenny crushed her against her bosom. "I'm so thrilled for you. You are such an artist with your cooking. And so talented."

Sophia frowned. "Elliott is talented."

Jenny rolled her eyes. "You're the one with the appeal, the presence in front of the camera. You charmed the heck out of us. You're a natural."

"But…" Sophia was interrupted by Mr. Smith.

"Sophia! We're so proud of you!" He pumped her hand enthusiastically. "I sure hope you'll consider doing some more programs with us. I honestly think you—and your daughters, too—would be a winning combination with the Creativity Channel. The three of you are fabulous on film."

"Mr. Smith, thank you but—"

For thirty more minutes Sophia was touched and crushed and congratulated. She witnessed genuine enthusiasm on some of the faces and envious looks as well. Chef Baldwin hugged her, and his hands lingered just a little too long near her breasts. She was too shocked to move. Tarquin and Jonathan were gracious and kind. All of the cast and crew included Cady and Emilia in their celebration, and Sophia was relieved to see her daughters smiling and relaxed.

But her eyes kept darting back to Elliott, who was playing the game to perfection. He laughed at the jokes and accepted well wishes from the contestants. But the tension lines on his face were tightening as the minutes crept by, and he started to avoid her gaze.

Finally, the celebration drew to a close, and Sophia watched Elliott walk away from the set. Alone.

"Cady, Emilia. I'll be right back." She hugged her daughters. "I need to speak to Elliott."

"Mom, do you think he's okay?" Emilia looked nervous. "I'm worried about him."

Cady nodded. "Me too."

"I'll take care of it." Sophia practically ran off the set, racing along the sidewalk on campus. She finally caught up with Elliott next to an enormous weeping willow near the dormitory.

She grabbed his arm. "Where do you think you're going? You're not even going to speak to me?" Tears poured down her cheeks. "You know this isn't right. I cannot accept this check when I know you're the chef who should have won."

"You won, Sophia. Not I."

"Not because my cooking was better."

Elliott ran a finger down her cheek. "I took a chance with the haggis. I wanted to showcase that Scottish specialty. I knew I was taking a chance, but my recipe is flawless. Too bad Jenny had a vote."

"You knew she had a vote. But you did it anyway."

"Aye, I did. What's done is done."

"I'm giving you the check."

His expression turned grim. "You are not. I will not accept it."

"Elliott, I don't need that money. You do. For your restaurant. Please, take it."

He shook his head. "No self-respecting Scot would stoop so low. I have my pride, woman. Spend that money on your sweet girls. They deserve it." He pulled away from her grip.

"No. Listen to me…" She tried to catch her breath.

"I heard the producers talking. About you and the girls and a concept for a new show. It sounds lovely. The three garden sprites and some mashed tomatoes." He pressed his lips against her forehead. "Do it. Take what they offer. This is a dream-of-a-lifetime. You said you wanted a fresh chance. Well, you got it. Don't pass this up."

"I don't want it." She blocked his path. "That's not *my* dream. I don't want a TV show."

"Don't be foolish, Sophia."

"I'm sure there are plenty of people who would jump at this chance, but it's not my dream, Elliott. I have dreams. Don't you want to know what they are?" She waited for his answer. Would he ask her? Would she tell him? Did she have enough courage to tell him?

He shook his head. "Sorry, Sprite, I don't have time. I have a lot on my plate right now." He smiled at her. A small, sad smile. "Uh-oh. Bad cooking pun. I think Mr. Smith is rubbing off on me." He leaned down and kissed her cheek, allowed his lips to linger there for a moment. "I need to get back to North Berwick and get my business in order."

"If they're going to do a cooking show, *you* should be the celebrity chef. Not me. You're the one with the talent." Sophia slid her arms around his waist and held onto him, afraid to let go.

"I never told you. So I'll tell you now." Elliott lifted her chin with one finger. "Your *amuse-bouche* was spectacular. It shocked the hell out of me. I couldn't believe that an amateur made that single bite. It was truly perfection. Heavenly. A taste of heaven, sweetheart. Every part of it. Even the flowers, love. Even the flowers."

"Elliott..." She couldn't stop the flow of tears now. He sounded so resigned to his fate. This wasn't right. "Let's talk about your predicament and figure it out. As a team. We can do this."

"No." He shook his head. "You are going to stay here with your girls, and I am going to head back to Scotland and take care of the mess I've made." He kissed her again.

She reveled in the feeling of his thick beard grazing her chin.

"I know you think your life has been blown to smithereens

with a big gaping hole, but I don't see it that way. I spent time with you and your daughters, and all I saw was a tight, loving family filled with joy. No hole. You are blessed." He grabbed onto her arms and physically lifted her away from his body. "Good-bye, Sophia. Congratulations."

He walked away.

 Chapter
Twenty-One

thought you told me your mother was doing better? She looks like a ghost." Mrs. Anderson's whispered concern floated over the hedges into the dark corner of Sophia's vegetable garden.

"She was doing better. But now..." Cady hesitated.

"She just needs some time, Mrs. Anderson. That's all. Time will heal her." Emilia's voice was firm.

"Sophia has had time. Over a year. And she looks like death. I know you girls are in college, but I honestly think you need some help. An adult to oversee your care, and her care. Perhaps Sophia's sister could come by for the rest of the summer."

"We are just fine, thank you. We're taking Mom on a big trip. All over the world. That will perk her up." Cady sounded like she was trying to convince herself.

"I'm not sure she's up for that, Cady. She looks like a strong wind would knock her over. A trip like that requires stamina—"

"Mrs. Anderson, it's time for lunch. If you don't mind, we need to talk with our mom. Alone." Emilia was using her no-nonsense voice.

Would it work on the old biddy? Sophia wondered.

"Very well. But I'll be back to check on you girls tomorrow."

"Don't bother. We'll be busy packing," Cady said.

Sophia finished her crown of violets and plopped it onto her head. She huddled in the corner of her garden with a bottle of Pinot Grigio, a cracked wine glass, and a wreath of flowers. The kind she used to fashion for the girls when they were little. She poked her fingernail into the skinny stem and threaded the next flower through until the blossom secured it in place. One after another, white violet, purple violet.

The garden fairy, drunk in the corner. The Big Winner. The big fraud. The lonely widow. Sprite. Beauty without her beast.

A trip around the world?

There was one place in the world she would visit. A little fishing village in southeast Scotland, twelve miles north of Dunbar. A seaside town with crumbling castles, lush beaches, and cramped townhouses overlooking the ocean. And somewhere, along the crowded streets, a restaurant on the brink of collapse, in a dark alley. With no light.

But with Elliott.

It was time to speak with her daughters about their itinerary.

◊ ◊ ◊

"What's this? It smells delicious." Sophia blinked at the bowl of soup in front of her.

"Cullen skink." Emilia handed her a spoon.

Sophia smiled. "The Scottish soup? How did you know how to make this, Em?"

"Googled it."

"When in doubt, Google that shit." Cady nodded like a wise old woman. She placed a cup of hot coffee in front of Sophia.

"Coffee and cullen skink. Thank you, girls." Sophia tasted the soup. It was wonderful, rich and creamy.

"Are you still drunk? We sort of need to talk," Cady said.

Sophia sighed. "No. Not drunk. Just tired."

Emilia sat down next to Sophia at their table. "Remember Plan B? The big trip around the world?"

"Yes. I was worried Plan B was electroshock therapy, but I'm relieved to hear it's a travel adventure. Much better."

"This isn't a joke." Cady's lower lip trembled. "It's not a joke!"

Emilia placed a comforting hand on her sister's arm. "Cady, it's okay. Mom, I don't care what it takes to make you better. Therapy, travel, medication—whatever it takes we're doing it."

Sophia placed the spoon on the mat next to her bowl. She slipped out of the chair and kneeled before her daughters. "I know you're not going to believe this, but I am feeling better. This is part of my better. I'm allowed to feel sorry for myself and pout in the garden for an afternoon. But my long-term grieving is over, girls. I will always miss your father. I will always have our memories. But I'm ready to move on. I'm ready to embrace the next phase of my life." She rested her cheek on Emilia's knee and her older daughter stroked her hair. Just the way Sophia used to stroke her baby's hair twenty years ago.

"Mommy, are you sure? You don't look so good." Cady wiped away her tears.

"I miss Elliott. I feel guilty and confused and frustrated. I think I might be falling in love with the grumpy Scottish bastard."

The girls laughed through their tears.

"We were wondering about that." Emilia lifted her mother's face.

Sophia smiled. "Yes, well, I've figured out a few things this past week. I'm finally ready to take some risks. Leave behind my quiet existence and take a chance on something big and bold and different. A new adventure. I loved my life with your father. But it's time to start over. Thank you for having faith in me. Thank you for signing me up for that show. I know I grumbled about it at the beginning. But you were right. I needed something to jostle me out of my depression."

"So are you okay to travel?" Cady asked. "We have a big list of possible destinations to discuss."

Sophia nodded. "I am. But I actually have a slightly different idea for Plan B. It's…a little bit crazy. And it might not work." She swallowed the nervous lump in her throat. "But I want to try. If it fails, it fails. But if it works, it could be astounding."

Sophia looked at her daughters' expectant faces. They both reached down to her and squeezed her shoulders.

"What's your Plan B, Mom? Tell us," Emilia said.

She told them.

# Chapter Twenty-Two

They stood at the top of North Berwick Law and gazed down at fields of brilliant yellow rapeseed. Like a carpet of gold spreading out to the sea. The wind tugged and pulled and pushed them. Whipped their curls across their faces, obscuring the view of the town and somewhere in the distance, Elliott Adamson.

Bass Rock rose up from the harbor, a lone chunk of volcanic rock. Not unlike Elliott himself. The lone rock, surrounded by choppy waters, stubborn and isolated and eerily beautiful as the sun set to the northwest.

Sophia lifted her arms and welcomed the wind. She felt battered, but she embraced the rush of air, pushing and tugging, leading her onto a new path. It was violent and exhilarating at the same time. Next to her, Emilia and Cady raised their arms in solidarity, and the three Brown women laughed into the wind. She imagined the currents stole their voices and carried them down the hill, across the golden fields, and into the narrow streets of the town.

❦ ❦ ❦

"Are we ready?" Sophia took a deep breath. The sign read S-one Soup. Even the sign was wrong, missing the "T," looking dingy and gray and sad.

"Jesus H. Christ," Cady said. "We've got our work cut out for us."

Emilia laughed. "He's going to pop an aneurysm when he sees us."

Sophia turned to her oldest daughter. "Remember when you said he needs us?"

Emilia nodded.

"You were right."

❦ ❦ ❦

Elliott was seated at a table in the middle of the room. He was smoking. A cigarette dangled from his lips, and he didn't even bother to turn around when they entered. An old man stood next to the bar and held a weathered cap in his hands.

"I'm sorry, ladies. We're closed today. Got some business to attend to."

Sophia nodded. "Are you Uncle Rory, by any chance?"

The old man smiled and shot them a near-toothless grin. "Aye, I am. And who are you, bonny lass?"

Elliott's shoulders tensed. He removed the cigarette from his mouth and smashed it into an ashtray on the table.

"Oh, Sophia, you chose the wrong day to visit, love." He still refused to turn around.

"Why is that, Elliott?" she asked. The restaurant stank like smoke and fish. It was small, cramped and dark. One of the most unwelcoming places she had ever seen in her life.

Elliott's shoulders hunched over. The beast looked withered and defeated. She wanted to wrap her arms around him from behind and ease his self-doubt and pain. Make him strong and arrogant and fearless again.

He let out a long, weary sigh. "Today is Death of a Restaurant, love. I've sold the place. Game over. You should have called first. I would have told you to save your money and go to Disney World instead."

"But I don't want to go to Disney World, Elliott. I wanted to come to Scotland. It's so irritating that you keep trying to tell me what I want, what I should do, what I ought to do." She took a deep breath. "I'm not a child. I can make up my own mind about things. Anyway, you didn't give me your phone number."

He barked out a laugh and finally turned around. When he saw Emilia and Cady at her side, he raised a brow. "Family trip? How cozy."

Sophia realized he was nursing a whisky already. At eight o'clock in the morning.

She walked over to the table and lifted the glass. "Uncle Rory, I think Elliott has had enough of this. Do you mind clearing the glass while I speak to him?"

Rory nodded. "You're the lass from the show, aren't you? Elliott told me about you, but he didn't tell me how bonny you are." He glanced at the girls behind her. "Are these your bairns?"

"Yes," Sophia answered. "Cady and Emilia."

"What a sweet family you have." He frowned at Elliott. "Don't mind my nephew. He's in a foul one today."

Sophia sat at the table. She ran her fingers down the side of Elliott's face, along the tough skin and thick beard, and along his lips. He nipped her.

"What do you think you're doing, love? This isn't the time and place for a seduction." He laughed. "Are you going to seduce me? I could use a spot of fun. This hasn't been the best week of my life."

"Why is that?" She continued to stroke his face.

He turned to inhale her wrist. Caught it in his own hand and held it still.

"Had to sell Stone Soup to pay off my creditors. I'm waiting for the new owners now. You and the girls should go. It's fucking humiliating enough without an audience." He reached for his glass, realized it was gone, and hollered, "Damn it, Rory! Where's my drink?"

She lifted both hands and cradled his angry face. "Elliott. Leave Uncle Rory alone. We need to talk. About the restaurant."

He shook his head. "Nothing left to talk about, sweet."

"Actually, there is. Meet your new boss." Sophia gestured to Emilia, and she stepped forward and held out a hand to Elliott.

"Chef Adamson, I've heard a lot about you."

Elliott's eyes darted back to Sophia, and then he started to chuckle. He laughed until he cried, and coughed, and then he finally pounded on the table.

"You didn't. Please, please, please tell me...you did not buy this wretched place. It's full of bad luck, you damned stupid American."

"Hey!" Cady hit Elliott on the shoulder. "Don't you call my mom stupid. You have no idea—"

"Cady, it's all right, honey." Sophia narrowed her eyes. "Elliott, this isn't a joke. You and I both know that you deserved to win that competition. You should have gotten the money, not I. But I realize now it's probably best you didn't get the cash yourself."

That got his attention. He sat up straighter in his chair and glared at her. "What the hell do you mean by that?"

"You can't just throw money at this place and think it will all work out. You need a total overhaul. New name, new venue, fresh start. Your cooking instincts are fabulous, but you need Cady running the front of the house, designing your space, bringing her sparkle and light into your project. You need Emilia managing the rest—the employees and wholesale accounts and thinking ahead. And planning promotional events."

Elliott rubbed a hand over his face and sighed. "Promotional events? Woman, you have lost your mind. I'm stuck here in this little town, and no one is bothering with me. Promotional events are not an issue."

"But in two months, you will be on the map, Elliott. In two months, *A Taste of Heaven* will air on television, and suddenly eager tourists will be searching for you and your restaurant. Excited to see the Beast in person and try his food."

"Try his haggis," Emilia said.

"And *his* delicious peach-rum trifle," Cady added. With her lop-sided smirk. "Although I fully expect that dessert to be named Cady's Kick-Ass Trifle."

"That show is going to change your life. You can either squander this opportunity and stay here in this dark little corner of North Berwick, or you can get your ass out of here. Emilia and I already found an excellent new location for the restaurant. We love this town. It's charming and lovely. You just need to choose wisely."

Elliott's nostrils flared. "Rory, could you please escort Cady and Emilia to the kitchen for a tour of these lovely facilities? I would like to have a word in private with Sophia."

"Of course." Uncle Rory gestured to the girls. "Right this way, ladies. Excuse the mess."

"Mom, are you okay?" Emilia took her mother's hand.

"Fine. Elliott and I need to talk."

Em nodded, and she and Cady left with Elliott's elderly uncle. Sophia watched them exit the restaurant through the back door, letting in a shaft of sunlight. And then the door slammed shut, leaving her and Elliott in the shadows.

"You just can't help yourself, Sophia. I'm like the baby bird in your garden. I've fallen out of the nest, and you have to nurse me back to health." Elliott shook his head slowly, simmering with anger. "Well, it's not going to work. You want to scrape me out of the bottom of the barrel. The three-time loser. And patch me up and make everything better. No, thank you. I'm done."

"But you keep making the same mistakes!" Sophia wanted to shake him. "You need to try something different this time.

Emilia and Cady and I are here. We are willing to try. You did it during the competition. You worked as a team, and it was successful. We need to start fresh, with a new concept."

"You're asking me to launch another new restaurant? I can't do it. I'm exhausted." His fatigue was etched all over his face. It broke her heart. The dark circles under his eyes. The stains on his rumpled shirt. The scent of whisky on his skin. He reeked of defeat.

"Don't you think I know what that feels like? The exhaustion? Trying to rustle up the energy to get out of bed every morning? I know. This time will be different."

"How so? How will this be different?"

"This time you have *me*." *Don't give up, Elliott. Not yet.*

He cupped her face with his callused hands. "I can't do it to you, love. You have no idea what you're getting into."

She shook her head, refusing to accept his words. "There are two ways to look at this. Two ways to look at life, Elliott. You can say '*Oh, I'm quitting again,*' or you can see it another way. That you have the courage to try something new. Take all the lessons you've learned in the last fifty years, embark on a fresh adventure, and learn to truly share the journey, the risks, and the failures instead of battling it out alone. This is exactly the same as *A Taste of Heaven*. We share the load. We blend the vision. We lean on each other. That's how a family works."

"Family." His voice was hoarse. "You don't think I'm jealous of what you have with those girls? Every time I see the three of you together I'm reminded that I never got around to having a family. Well, I *am* jealous. And yes, I have regrets. I made sacrifices for my professional career, and look where it's gotten me." Elliott rubbed his eyes. "Sweetheart, take your girls and go."

"No." Sophia trembled with frustration. "No, I will *not* go. Where is the man who butchered the turkeys? Who was fearless? Cocky? Where is he? I'm not leaving." She reached for his hand and squeezed it. Her heart was pounding with fear. Why wasn't Elliott listening to her?

He stared at their fingers locked together and sighed. "You realize that this time my failure will be broadcast all over the world? You're proposing a huge undertaking. And as you pointed out, I'll soon be on the map. Which means this new project will be in the spotlight. If I fail—if *we* fail—everyone will know."

"We won't fail."

He shook his head. "Sophia…"

"I believe in me. And in you. And in my daughters. And Uncle Rory. We will *not* fail."

Elliott narrowed his eyes and then shifted in his seat. She saw something flicker in his indigo gaze, something…curious. Hopeful.

Be brave, Elliott.

"And what about you and your future career in television? Mr. Smith must be breathing down your neck."

"If Mr. Smith wants to film *our* new venture, we can discuss that later. But right now we have a restaurant to get off the ground in the next two months. Before that show changes our lives. Did you even read the contract you signed? You agreed to cook for the new owner for at least a year."

Elliott groaned. "Hell, no. I didn't read the fine print."

Emilia and Cady walked back into the restaurant. "Don't worry about it, Chef Adamson. I'll take care of contracts from now on." Emilia perched on a bar stool and stared down at him.

"There is no way this…*kid*…who is barely out of her twenties is going to be bossing me around. No. Damned. Way." Elliott pounded the table.

"Too late. You already signed the contract. This kid is smart and savvy. And that kid"—she pointed at Cady—"is creative and filled with enthusiasm. They are exactly the kind of people you want involved in a project like this. You have the experience and cooking talent. And we have the inspiration for a new start. No more working alone, in a vacuum, without a sounding board or alternate opinions. It's time for a team effort. With people who care about you and are invested in this place. Invested in *you*." Sophia looked down at her feet. "Yes, we are taking a risk. But it's worth a shot, Elliott. You are such a gifted chef. It would be a horrible shame if the world didn't get to see what you're capable of. Please. Let's just try."

Elliott rubbed the top of his head. "You have lost your mind. What about your old life? Your home in Vermont? The girls are still in college. You're just going to chuck it all and take a chance on this? Are you daft?"

"The cottage will always be there. But I'm ready for a change, a new adventure. I know I'm strong enough to do this. And the girls are on board."

Elliott's gaze wandered from her to Cady and Em. "What about school?"

"We're taking a leave of absence. And might transfer to a Scottish university. We wanted to be part of Mom's Plan B." Cady slid her arm around Sophia's shoulder.

Rory leaned down and whispered into Elliott's ear. "Listen to the bonny gals. I think we need a feminine touch around here. And they seem to know what they're talking about."

Elliott stood and swayed. He shook his head and then hauled Sophia up on her feet. "I wish I hadn't been drinking this morning. Let's see if I have this straight. You and your busy-body, interfering offspring have bought my restaurant. And I have to cook for you for at least a year. Is that right?"

Sophia nodded. "You're half-owner, Elliott. If you'd bothered to read the contract, you would have seen that. The Brown family owns half. You own half. You and I won that contest together, as a pair. Fifty-fifty contribution. The money was ours to split. I just fixed things so it worked out that way."

He turned to glare at the girls. "I'm afraid to find out what your plans are for this *'new'* adventure."

"Glad you asked!" Cady chirped. "We already found the perfect space, two streets down. It's light and inviting. We'll be open for dinner only, lunch on the weekends."

"Four or five Scottish specialties per dinner, to really showcase the traditional food you love to cook," Emilia said. "Seating for about twenty-five to thirty. A small, intimate space."

Elliott's face began to turn red. "You have no—"

"And no more uncomfortable wooden chairs," Cady said, ignoring him. She banged her fist on the seat and cringed. "Jesus. This is like a prison bench. We'll have comfortable furniture. The space will be simply decorated, with fresh flowers on all the tables."

Elliott rolled his eyes. "Oh, I can only imagine the flowers. You're planning to turn my new restaurant into a garden. Of course you are."

Sophia crossed her arms. "Is your ego too big to share the spotlight with us, Chef Adamson? To work as a team this time, instead of alone?"

She and her daughters waited for his response. His eyelid twitched. She knew that look on his face. The one he got when he was assessing things, mentally exploring his options.

He frowned at her. "I'm not quite sure whose dream this really is. Mine? Or yours, Sophia? Is this the Forget-Me-Not Café, Scottish version? You have no idea how difficult it is to run a real restaurant. That show was for entertainment. Running a business is fraught with risk. You sure you can handle that? Are you sure you can handle *me*?"

She stepped closer to Elliott and smiled. He wasn't afraid of a new restaurant. He was afraid of becoming part of a family. He was insecure about her.

Whose dream is this?

"You told me to be selfish, to take and take and take. Remember?"

His nostrils flared. "Aye. I remember, love."

"I'm being selfish."

"This is you being selfish? Giving away your prize money to me is you being *selfish*?" He barked out a laugh.

"I want to open a restaurant with you. I want to cook with you. I want to *be* with you. Yes, this is me being selfish."

Whose dream is this? This is my dream. Finally crawling out of that dark cave. Searching for light. For lightness and joy again. Revisiting forgotten dreams and inviting someone to share them with me.

"Yes, I can handle it. And of course I can handle you. You forget who I am. The fierce, strong-willed competitor. Remember?"

She was desperate to touch him and remind him. To feel the comforting sensation of his heated skin against her. But first she had to convince him about their future.

Elliott leaned down to look her in the eye. "You're sure? You're making me feel like a coward. I keep running away. And here you are, halfway across the world, running toward something. I don't know if I'd have the guts to do it."

"You're running toward something too, Elliott. A family. Friends you can count on. This loner business isn't working out for you. You've been adopted by the Brown Family. Whether you like it or not."

"And we adopted Uncle Rory, too," Cady said. She linked arms with the old man, who was trying to hide his tears.

Emilia slipped off the stool and approached Elliott. "This venture is not about you. And it's not about mom. It's about blending traditions. The Adamson family and the Brown family. We're making something new. Uncle Rory, what's your favorite thing about Elliott's restaurant?"

Rory looked startled. "Well, I'd have to say I enjoy the ale. Elliott has the best selection from the UK."

Emilia nodded. "So we have Rory's Choice every night on the menu. And Cady's Spotlight Dessert. And mom will have a vegetarian dish. And you'll have your Scottish specialties, and all these things will work together. They just will."

"Woven together like a blanket," Elliott whispered.

Sophia leaned against his chest. "Yes."

"This is crazy. Three bossy American women who have no restaurant experience at all. One eighty-two-year-old man who loves his ale. And a three-time loser. Christ." Elliott closed his eyes.

"Maybe we need some crazy," Sophia answered gently.

Elliott opened his eyes and buried his face in her neck. "What about us, sweetheart? You came all this way to save my arse. You know I fell for you on the very first day you gave me attitude on that show. I tried to dismiss you, and you almost combusted right there. You flashed your fire at me, and I was smitten on the spot. I could tell there was something special about you. And I was right."

She stroked his bald head and kissed his ear. "You fell for me?"

"You know I did. I don't think I can watch you flirt with every man who walks into our place. Torture myself with that."

"Would it be torture?" she asked.

"Aye. And since I would slug them and end up in jail, our restaurant probably wouldn't last too long."

She laughed against his chest.

"Tell me. Have you fallen in love with this stubborn Scottish chef?" Elliott tipped up her chin. He wouldn't let her hide anymore.

"Yes." Simple, direct. The new Sophia was not afraid.

"You promise you won't run away from me? What if this doesn't work out? Will I lose my sweet garden fairy? I'm worried you'll slip through my fingers and run off through the forest. I don't want to lose you." He swallowed, and the fear glistened in his eyes.

"Oh, Elliott. I'm not running away. Never running away, no matter what happens with the restaurant. I ran *to* you. Why do you think I'm here?" She slid her arms around his neck, pulling him closer, finally taking his heat and his love. He tightened the circle of his arms around her, trying to lock her in place.

All of the tension eased from his big body, and he smiled. That brilliant, cocky smile. The one that showed her the old Elliott was roaring back to life. Stubborn Elliott. Infuriating Elliott. Sexy Elliott.

She glanced over her shoulder at Emilia and Cady. And Uncle Rory. And she felt the final threads pull taut, closing up the gaping wound. This was her family. This was her future.

Elliott leaned his forehead against hers. "I have a good idea for a name. For the new place." His eyes sparkled with mischief. He started to laugh.

And then they all were laughing. Elliott and Uncle Rory—still teary-eyed—and her two daughters, perched on the bar stools.

Elliott kissed her.

He tasted like whisky.

He tasted like hope.

He tasted like heaven.

 Epilogue

One year later...

Restaurant Review
WIFE NUMBER FOUR
North Berwick Daily News
Review by Alistair MacDaniel

What a difference a year makes!

One year ago, Chef Elliott Adamson's restaurant, Stone Soup, was on the chopping block—for good reason. As my readers know, I sampled the wares at this small cramped establishment on several occasions, and the food was, at best, inconsistent. The atmosphere was, at worst, horrid (see issues 32-14 and 59-14 in the Daily News). After a string of failed enterprises, the future was not looking cheery for Chef Adamson.

Until *A Taste of Heaven* aired.

That's right. Our very own Chef Adamson participated

in the highly popular TV show produced by the Creativity Channel. Adamson and thirteen other contestants battled it out in the quaint state of Vermont for $50,000. Although Adamson made it to the finals, he did not win. His partner, the lovely Sophia Brown, emerged as the victor. But in a stunning series of events, she and Elliott became business partners for his fourth eatery. WIFE NUMBER FOUR has since put North Berwick on the culinary map.

I dined there on three separate occasions, alone and with friends. We were pleasantly surprised by the menu, the atmosphere, and the camaraderie within this fine restaurant. Although Chef Adamson and I came close to fisticuffs after my last review (in issue 98-14 of the Daily News), he was welcoming on all recent visits.

The hostess, Miss Cady Brown, is a bit cheeky. When questioned about her responsibilities at WIFE NUMBER FOUR, she told me her official title was "Master of the Universe." I'm still not sure if she was being sarcastic.

Restaurant manager Emilia Brown is doing a superb job. The menu is eclectic, the wait staff is attentive and polite, and the interior of the restaurant is comfortable and stylish.

Favorite dishes include Scottish specialties such as Cullen Skink and Chef Adamson's signature Haggis with Pancetta. There are some new items on the menu as well, including a hearty Seafood Risotto and a delicate pasta dish—Sophia's Linguine with Cream Sauce. Everything was seasoned perfectly and garnished with fresh herbs and whimsical flowers. The dessert menu was most impressive. Miss Cady Brown made a point to inform us she inspired the Peach Shortbread Trifle.

It was refreshing to see Chef Adamson with a smile on his face. He visited all the tables to inquire about our meals and chatted amicably with the patrons. I also noticed he could not keep his hands off the lovely Sophia Brown—which she didn't seem to mind in the least.

When I questioned part-owner "Uncle Rory" about Chef Adamson's change of attitude, he just winked at me and pointed to Ms. Brown.

Chef Brown is even more adorable in person than on television. I do believe it's Sophia's warmth and enthusiasm that imbue this bistro with its charm and personality. During all of our visits, she was beaming with happiness.

My overall impression of WIFE NUMBER FOUR: spectacular. I highly recommend this delightful restaurant. And if you'll forgive the horrible pun, it was certainly a "taste of heaven."

All my best,
Alistair MacDaniel

About the Author

PENNY WATSON is a native Pittsburgher whose love of romance started at the age of twelve when she discovered *Gone With The Wind* in the middle school library. This resulted in numerous attempts at a first novel involving a young lady with windswept hair who lived in a tree house.

A biologist by training, Penny has worked at various times as a dolphin trainer, science teacher, florist, and turf grass researcher (don't ask). After taking time off to raise her two spirited children, she decided to rekindle her passion for storytelling. Now she gets to incorporate her wide array of interests—including gardening, cooking, and travel—into her works of fiction.

Penny lives outside of Boston with one fly-fishing crazed husband, two lively Filipino kids, and a wiener dog.

Please visit Penny's website *www.pennyromance.com* for more information about her upcoming releases and to sign up for her newsletter.

Also by Penny Watson

APPLES SHOULD BE RED

"Hilarious and sweet, a delightfully romantic gem of a story."
-- Laura Florand, Bestselling author of *The Chocolate Series*

2015 Colorado RWA Award of Excellence Finalist
2015 DABWAHA Finalist
One of the "Best Romance Novels in 2014" at About.com

Recipe for Thanksgiving Dinner:

Start with sixty-two year old politically incorrect, chain-smoking, hard-cussing curmudgeon.
Add fifty-nine year old sexually-repressed know-it-all in pearls.
Throw in a beer can-turkey, a battle for horticultural supremacy, and nudist next-door neighbor.
Serve on paper plates, garnished with garden gnome.
Tastes like happily ever after.

Penny Watson presents an over-fifty romantic comedy novella. 21,000 words. Story includes copious profanity and botanical references.

Available in print and ebook at Amazon, Barnes and Noble, and Kobo

THE KLAUS BROTHERS SERIES

"SWEET MAGIK will surely help readers get into the Christmas

spirit...suspend disbelief and go along for a ride to the North Pole."
-- RT Book Reviews

What if the legend of Santa Claus is real? What if Santa has five strapping sons who help him run his empire? Five single, sexy sons looking for romance?

SWEET INSPIRATION – Klaus Brothers Series #1

Nicholas Klaus is a master pastry chef, a strict disciplinarian, and the eldest son of the legendary Santa Claus. One look at café owner Lucy Brewster sends him into an unexpected tailspin of lusty desires. When Lucy is injured, Nicholas makes a decision that catapults both of their lives into turmoil...

Lucy Brewster, the free-spirited proprietor of Sweet Inspiration, has a flair for concocting sugary confections but no time for adventure. She gets more than she bargained for when she awakens in the North Pole...rambunctious elves, a fitness-obsessed Santa, and the man of her dreams.

Does she have what it takes to become the next Mrs. Klaus?

Available in print and ebook at Amazon, Barnes and Noble, and Kobo

SWEET MAGIK – Klaus Brothers Series #2

"To borrow a little German, this book was wunderbar."
-- Romancing Rakes

Oskar Klaus' job is killing him. Not even his favorite hobbies (extreme snowboarding and browsing old bookstores) are enough to snap him out of his funk. It's not easy living in the shadow of four successful older brothers and a father named Santa. Little does he know that a kiss on New Year's Eve is about to turn his life upside-down.

Kiana Grant's Manhattan life is a world away from her childhood in Oahu. She traded sunsets and surfing for a respectable career in library science, but Oskar Klaus is a temptation that's hard to resist. Before she knows it, she's in the midst of an outrageous adventure in the North Pole, dealing with mischievous elves, wicked demons, and a devastating attraction to Santa's youngest son.

There's just one problem...a bitter elf hell-bent on revenge threatens the future of everyone in the North Pole, even Santa himself...

Available in print and ebook at Amazon, Barnes and Noble, and Kobo

SWEET ADVENTURE – Klaus Brothers Series #3

"Fans of the Klaus Brothers books will eat this one up."
-- Babbling About Books

Sven Klaus, Chief Toy Designer for Klaus Enterprises, will protect his family at any cost. He's prepared to battle the most threatening adversaries to do it—frost flowers, snowstorms, Yeti. And beautiful tenacious tabloid journalists.

Andi De Luca's reporting career is built on lies—about corrupt politicians, greedy Hollywood stars, and Bigfoot. Now she's determined to uncover the truth about Klaus Enterprises, and she always gets her story. Even if it means revealing her own secret desires to Santa's son.

After all the lies and deception are exposed, will Andi and Sven survive this North Pole adventure? Or will YETI MAKE THEM DEADY?

Penny Watson presents a 45,000-word holiday romance novella, #3 in the Klaus Brothers Series. Includes paranormal phenomena, Christmas spirit, and yes…an abominable snowmonster.

SWEET ADVENTURE can be read as a stand-alone story.

Available in print and ebook at Amazon, Barnes and Noble, and Kobo

LUMBERJACK IN LOVE

"The delicious beard! The magnificent log!
This city-girl-meets-lumberjack tale is a crazy sexy hairy delight."
-- Carolyn Crane, author of The Disillusionists Trilogy

City slicker Ami Jordan was just dumped by her backstabbing boyfriend, has no job prospects, and can't find a decent cup of coffee in the entire state of Vermont. The last thing she needs is a sexy, bearded lumberjack complicating her life. Even if he's smart, talented, and has the hottest ass she's ever seen.

Tree house builder, environmental champion, and Bulldog owner Marcus Anderson has no patience for flatlanders with an attitude. But when landscape designer Ami Jordan shows up at his log cabin, he suddenly develops a hankering for a high-maintenance city gal. Now his house looks like a jungle, his recycling is in disarray, and his libido's on fire.

He's a lumberjack in love.

Available in print and ebook at Amazon, Barnes and Noble, and Kobo

Download the free epilogue for LUMBERJACK IN LOVE
Go to *www.pennyromance.com* for the link!

Check out the children's series by Nina Clark and Sara Pulver...

LUCY THE WONDER WEENIE!

"Lucy is sure to tickle the funny bones of young kids and wiener dog-lovers of all ages. The bright, charmingly wacky illustrations build the perfect world for a wiener dog with a newly-found superpower."
-- Pam Smallcomb, author of EARTH TO CLUNK

Lucy the Diva Doxie irritates her family with an obsessive licking habit. Then one day she consumes a pile of magic beans and something extraordinary happens. She transforms into LUCY THE WONDER WEENIE. After adopting her new super hero persona, Lucy makes a startling discovery. Her bothersome habit has the power to comfort tearful children and create laughter, love, and joy.

Because every dog's a superhero.

Available in print and ebook at Amazon, Barnes and Noble, and Kobo

Check out the Wonder Weenie website at
www. lucythewonderweenie.blogspot.com.

Made in the USA
Middletown, DE
30 September 2015